When Mary Grey hears that Harriet West has been arrested for murder in the beautiful and quaint French town of Munier they take the next train out. To their shock, Harriet confesses to the killing but swears it was self-defense. As they try to piece together the truth, more than one skeleton is unearthed in this seemingly sleepy community.

PERIL IN PROVENCE

The Mary Grey Mysteries, Book Four

Winnie Frolik

A NineStar Press Publication

www.ninestarpress.com

Peril in Provence

© 2024 Winnie Frolik

Cover Art © 2024 Jaycee DeLorenzo

This is a work of fiction. Names, characters, places, and incidents are either the product of the author's imagination or are used fictitiously. Any resemblance to actual persons living or dead, business establishments, events, or locales is entirely coincidental.

All rights reserved. No part of this publication may be reproduced in any material form, whether by printing, photocopying, scanning or otherwise without the written permission of the publisher. To request permission and all other inquiries, contact NineStar Press at the physical or web addresses above or at Contact@ninestarpress.com.

First Edition, September 2024

ISBN: 978-1-64890-799-9

Also available in eBook, ISBN: 978-1-64890-798-2

CONTENT WARNING:
This book contains language reflecting the attitudes of the time, murder, references to suicide, anti-Semitism, and xenophobic slurs.

PROLOGUE

Provence, October 28, 1937

The weather could not have been better for the Feast of St. Simon and St. Jude. The day dawned bright and sunny without a cloud in the too-blue sky and only the gentlest of breezes. Yes, there was an autumnal chill, but it was a briskness that enlivened and stirred the blood rather than keeping people indoors. It had been many years since the Feast Day had enjoyed such pleasant treatment from the elements. Throughout the day, the town square was filled with prize-laden raffle stands selling wines and cheeses. Rounds of boules were played with a level of intensity unseen since the days of duels. This year's festivities had coincided with the arrival of several Gypsy caravans to the area, and they displayed such carnival acts as knife throwing and fire swallowing. A self-proclaimed seer set up a tent to read tarot cards, and soon a long line formed as all the girls in town waited to learn who their future husband would be. Fronsac, the local artist, made numerous sketches of everything he saw, imagining a new series of oils he would paint commemorating pastoral gaiety. Day became night, but the mood remained merry. The moon itself shone that night with golden radiance. So of course, some form of wickedness had to come along and ruin it. C'est la vie.

All this was quite obvious to everyone in hindsight, but initially on the evening in question, the mood was one of gaiety—even jubilation. For Munier, like all such villages, adored its fêtes votives.

Per tradition, the Feast was held in the town square. A small stage with a microphone had been set up where Mayor Farigoule gave his annual speech, followed by two of the local chevaliers. They spoke at length on the joys of community, fellowship, and the excellent harvest season that year as anxious toes tapped impatiently.

The local priest reminded everyone of the spiritual nature of the occasion; St Jude and St. Simon were two of the original apostles and Jesus's own cousins who would attain martyrdom in Persia. "Do not forget," Father Benedict instructed, "that glorious St. Jude is the Patron Saint of Lost Causes," before offering prayers and blessing.

Finally, all the fine oratory ended, and the true business of gluttony could commence as dinner was served. People sat wherever they could find seats. Madame Dellaire of the chateau and her nephew Maxim sat side by side with the peasants who worked her estate and their wives. The owner of one of the finest local vineyards dined alongside one of the area's most infamous truffle poachers. The former had at one time threatened to shoot the latter if he ever caught him on his property. But for tonight at least, all was forgiven and the two happily broke bread together. Literally. They each grabbed a different end of a baguette, tearing it in two. Neighborhood dogs eagerly scampered below the tables, picking up scattered morsels and tossed bones. Neighborhood cats kept watchful eyes out from the alleys for the rats and other vermin who'd inevitably be attracted by the feast's detritus.

And what a feast it was! Long trestle tables of

rough planked wood groaned under the weight of their offerings: cheeses, baguettes, olive oil by the jug, canapés, bouillabaisse, rosemary-flavored chicken, roasted baby lamb with a creamy garlic sauce, and loins of pork stuffed with mushrooms. One platter even held a freshly caught wild sanglier, roasted and served with an apple in its mouth. And of course there was wine. It had been a fine year for the local grape growers, and in good Gallic tradition, everyone was now enjoying the fruits of their labor. Reds and whites seemed to flow endlessly at the table. It brought color to the English lady's cheeks, and she talked faster. The young American polished off one drink only to find another thrust into his hands, seemingly out of nowhere, to enjoy. The two of them were a familiar enough sight—the English lady who regularly visited the local boulangerie and the American gentleman who was fond of taking country drives at lightning speed.

"Now this is why I love France!" he roared out to the crowd as he quaffed his glass before making a face. That, he thought, had not been one of the region's better vintages.

Beside the stage and tables, another area had been cleared for the dancing that must always follow such a feast. By some miracle, people who moments earlier had been almost comatose through overindulgence were now on their feet and moving. An old white-haired Gypsy played the fiddle while his pretty young granddaughter danced with a tambourine. Monsieur Picard as per usual brought out his prized accordion. Many traditional old favorites were played, then the fiddler struck up the paso doble. Gaston the local innkeeper declined all attempts to cajole him to dance, preferring to instead sit on the sidelines and drink. There were plenty of others, though, who were happy to rise to the occasion. The barmaid danced with the local gendarme. The town butcher paired off with the baker's daughter. Maxim gallantly offered his arm to the local schoolteacher to let her have a turn. Mayor Farigoule gallantly led Madame Dellaire in an impromptu waltz that earned a round of applause from all, including the mayor's young wife Monique, who sadly could not dance that evening due to a sore toe. She, like Monsieur Duval the town's pharmacist, watched the dancing from the sidelines.

Curiously, the American and Englishwoman were not there. Perhaps they did not like dancing. And then a couple of people felt drops of rain. Within a matter of seconds, the sprinkle became a torrent, and everyone was struggling to find shelter under the tents and newspapers. Farmers and gentry alike shook their heads glumly, not just for the end of the evening's festivities but for what it meant to the broader climate. These were not the rains of summer with fat, warm, lazy droplets. No, these were the cold, pounding sheets of water that signaled the arrival of winter. Such floodwaters could sweep away entire fields and level streets as surely as a mine detonating. Worse yet, with the rain, they could feel the wind begin to change. The mistral had arrived once more in all its terrible glory. Uneaten crumbs of cheese and scraps of bread from the tables became airborne and blew among décolletage and shirt fronts. Tablecloths snapped and billowed like sails in full wind. Wineglasses and candles tipped over, and there was a moment's concern for a possible fire when another disaster entirely intervened.

"Regardez!" a young boy called out, pointing above, and all eyes turned. Munier's rampart walls, built over seven centuries ago, stood two stories high and along them lay a narrow path lined with a parapet. It had become almost as well trodden over the years as the city cobblestones. Atop those ramparts now were two figures. One male. One female. The latter had his arms around the former. Some in the crowd may have recognized the figures in question as being the foreign guests of Madame Dellaire. The American and the English-woman.

Normally, the sight of them out on a moonlit night together in physical engagement would signal an affaire de coeur. But this was no romantic liaison. Indeed, the two of them appeared to be yelling at each other, though their voices could not be made out from below. Some would later claim the woman's face was contorted with unearthly rage. Others would say she looked frightened. Then there were those who freely admitted to being too far away to really see her face, but they didn't get much attention. Honesty never makes for riveting testimony. What everyone from the square could see, however, was that the woman tore herself from the arms of the man with a heavy shove.

What was the purpose of the push? Was it, as the woman would later maintain, simply to get away? Was it an act of adrenaline? Or was it, as others would later charge, a deliberate act of malice? There would be a great deal of argument later about intention. It is truly remarkable how willingly people who have never claimed the gift of clairvoyance in the past would be in this instance to assert with full confidence that they—and they alone—knew to have been in the minds of the persons on the wall that night!

What no one could dispute was the result. When the woman pushed him, the man stumbled back on the parapet of the rampart wall...and went over. For one eternal moment, he seemed permanently suspended in the air. His mouth gaped open in shock, and his arms stretched up above him as if reaching for a rope to grab onto. Then gravity overtook him. The man hit the cobblestone street below with a sickening thud and a thick pool of dark liquid began pouring underneath his head. There was a moment of shocked silence.

Then came the screams.

CHAPTER ONE

October 30, 1937

Much to Shaefer's bemusement, Mary insisted on carving a turnip for All Hallows' Eve. It wasn't, as Mary was the first to admit, the cleanest or most artistic of efforts, but still, she took great pride in lighting it up and putting it in the little back window.

As she and Shaefer admired their effort, they heard a knock on the door. "Telegram for Mr. Shaefer," a voice announced.

"Shall I?" Mary asked. Shaefer was in his slippers listening to the radio.

"Ja!" He gestured.

Mary hurriedly answered the door to find an adenoidal youth holding out a wire message. She grabbed it, and as she read it, her face contorted.

"What is it?" Shaefer asked.

"It's Harriet. She's been arrested for murder." Mary read on. "In France! She's sitting in a prison down there right now."

Most people upon hearing that a close personal acquaintance has been charged with murder would be overcome with shock. They'd find themselves at a loss for what to do. Mary Grey and Franz Shaefer, however, were not most people. The latter was a professional private investigator and the former his assistant and apprentice. They were certainly surprised by the notion; neither had ever known Harriet West to exhibit any kind of homicidal tendency. But it wasn't quite the jolt to them as it would have been for anyone else. Shaefer in his years as a police detective in Berlin had been mixed up in countless murder investigations, and within the last year, Mary had gotten entwined in several as well.

Within an hour of receiving the telegram, the two of them were packed and on the way to catch the overnight ferry train to Paris. They took the unprecedented indulgence of booking a first-class sleeping compartment, reasoning that Harriet would almost certainly pay them back. She was, after all, a great heiress and quite a generous one at that. They also ordered freely off the dining car menu, though neither of them spoke much at dinner and they scarcely noticed their dishes. They were both lost in their own thoughts.

Almost a year earlier, Harriet had hired Shaefer to bring her brother's killer to justice. He had done so, and her fee had helped him get his sister and her family out of Germany and sent safely on to New Zealand. Another, more unexpected result of the matter had been that Harriet West and Mary Grey fell in love. Hard to know what had been more improbable about the pairing—that Harriet and Mary were both women or the difference in social stature. Harriet was one of the wealthiest and most desirable socialites in England. Mary was the daughter of a seamstress and, at the time she and Harriet had met, had been employed as a district nurse. But for a few months anyway, they'd lived together in a fragile sort of Eden. Of course, inevitably Paradise had been lost and Mary had gone on to work for Shaefer while Harriet had run off to France.

Shaefer, knowing all this, worried about Mary. She and Harriet had separated only a short time ago. She'd hardly had time to get over her heartbreak, and this reunion was bound to stir up a lot of emotions. Criminal investigations required cool, impartial logic. He already knew Mary wasn't going to be able to muster any of that here. But he also knew trying to prevent Mary from coming along would have been a hopeless cause.

Mary herself wasn't sure exactly how she felt. She was caught between anxiety for Harriet's future, anger at Harriet for leaving her in the first place, smugness that Harriet had in fact called on her in a time of crisis— well, her and Shaefer anyway. She couldn't bear the thought of seeing Harriet again. She couldn't wait to see Harriet again! It was like a pair of birds had taken up residence in her chest and were now pecking each other to death.

How would it feel to see Harriet again? She didn't know. She couldn't know until she actually saw Harriet. Yet knowing it was no use trying to dwell on the matter couldn't stop her from doing so. It was as frustrating a situation as one could be in, and it was only after a great deal of tossing and turning that Mary achieved any sleep.

*

They arrived in Paris shortly after breakfast. Shaefer had traveled there before, but it was Mary's first time. In fact, it was the first time Mary had ever been out of England at all. This was the very year the Paris Expo was being held, and under different circumstances, Mary would have been anxious to see it, particularly the Spanish pavilion with its supposedly shocking painting *Guernica* by that Picasso fellow. But there was simply no time to visit the Expo or to see any of the sights of Paris at all. Rather, a phone call to Harriet's solicitors in England had gotten them money wired on credit as well as the name of a prominent Parisian attorney, Jean François Jorisse, who wanted to meet them. They immediately hailed a cab, and so all Mary saw of Paris were a few glimpses through the window of a speeding vehicle.

Jorisse's offices lay in a quiet, yet prosperous-looking street of limestone buildings overhung with crawling ivy. Shaefer and Mary walked up a flight of dimly lit stairs to ring a buzzer, then down a corridor to a young woman at a reception desk. An extremely chic, fashionable young woman who wore an expression of determined ennui. She said nothing but with a tilt of her head indicated Mary and Shaefer could go in through an unlocked door. This led them into Jorisse's office, a good-sized room decorated in a surprisingly modern style with sleek Danish furniture. On the wall hung several frighteningly abstract paintings made up of dark colors, squiggly lines, and no recognizable shapes. It was exactly the sort of art that Harriet had favored and which Mary had never quite understood the point of.

Jorisse was a distinguished-looking man of about fifty years of age with a heavyset figure, silver hair at his temples, and a perfectly trimmed mustache and beard. His suit was well tailored, and he smelled of expensive perfume. Well, technically it was called "cologne" rather than perfume, but what Jorisse wore was a finer and more flowery scent than you'd ever catch being worn by most British women let alone men. One could also tell at first glance that unlike any British lawyer there was no possible circumstance in which Jorisse would ever wear tweed. Nor did he seem the sort of fellow you could prevail on for a round of golf or, indeed, any rigorous outdoor activity at all. One modern trend Jorisse fiercely resisted was the cult of physical exercise.

"Bonjour," he greeted them, holding out a manicured hand for Shaefer to shake. "Your reputation precedes you, Monsieur Shaefer."

"You've heard of me?" Shaefer was pleasantly surprised by both the cordiality of the greeting and the firmness of the handshake.

"But of course! Even in Paris, we have heard all about the great detective Franz Shaefer." Jorisse smiled.

"It is an honor to meet you in person!" He added as a clear afterthought, "And you too, Mademoiselle...Grey? I did pronounce it correctly?"

"You did," Mary confirmed.

"I understand Harriet West contacted both of you," Jorisse continued thoughtfully, examining Mary. For while Shaefer's presence was understandable, Mary Grey was something of a riddle, one he couldn't quite unravel.

"Miss Grey is my dear friend and associate," Shaefer cut in smoothly. "She was also involved in the investigation into the death of Anthony West last winter."

"Ah, of course." Jorisse smiled. "That explains it! But where are my manners? Both of you sit! Get comfortable." They both did sit, though neither could do so with any degree of comfort in the modern Danish chairs.

"What do you know so far?" Jorisse began.

"Absolutely nothing, except that Miss West was just arrested for murder and that she has retained you as local counsel," Shaefer responded.

Mary broke in, "Now whatever the hell is going on? How can Harriet be accused of murder in some place called Muh-neer?"

"Non, it is pronounced Munier," Jorisse gently

corrected her. "Now, the facts are quite simple. As you may have known, Miss West spent considerable time this summer in the French Riviera, primarily in Cannes. It was there she met Madame Hortense Dellaire. The Dellaires are a very old, very proud family in Provence. It seems that she and Harriet West became quite friendly and Madame Dellaire invited her to an extended visit at her family chateau near the medieval town of Munier. Miss West was not the only guest Madame Dellaire invited, or even the only foreigner. There was an American journalist, Bill Holbrook." He paused significantly. "It is he who Mademoiselle West killed."

"Don't you mean allegedly killed?" Mary rebuked sharply.

"Non." He shook his head firmly. "Did kill. She pushed him off a high wall and he died. It happened in front of dozens of witnesses, and Mademoiselle West has already freely admitted to the deed. As I said, the facts of the case could not be simpler. The only thing in dispute is whether she was justified in her actions or not."

There was a long pause.

"I don't understand," Mary began, feeling as if her head had been pounded by a brick. Harriet a murderess? It couldn't be! Could it?

"Mademoiselle West claims that in the moments

before his death, Monsieur Holbrook was, and I quote, 'acting like a madman.' That he was yelling absurdities and physically assaulted her," Jorisse recited in a calm tone. "He allegedly grabbed her by the shoulders and was issuing vague threats. Mademoiselle West claims that in her fear she pushed him solely to get away from him, and that his subsequent fall and demise were completely unintentional."

"Self-defense then," Mary interrupted with palpable relief. "Of course! That's what happened!"

Jorisse arched an eyebrow. "That is what Mademoiselle West says happened. But the local gendarmes are not so sure. Mademoiselle West and Monsieur Holbrook had been seen a great deal in each other's company in the weeks since they'd arrived at the chateau. The monsieur had a reputation for being popular with the ladies. Some say the two were lovers."

"They do?" Mary asked more sharply than intended. "I mean, were they or weren't they?"

Jorisse gave a Gallic shrug. "Who knows? They were supposed to be on familiar terms yet English-women in my experience are so cold and reserved," he opined, seemingly oblivious to Mary's presence. She wasn't offended but rather bemused. "But the point is the gendarmes, they hear all this, and they wonder if this could have been a crime passionnel."

"Of course they would," Mary grumbled bitterly. "Always looking for the most lurid explanation for everything."

"Oui, a love of drama perhaps influences them," Jorisse agreed. "Also, Miss West is English." He added this part with grave emphasis.

"So?" Mary responded, incredulous. "What's that got to do with anything?"

"It means that as Miss West is a foreigner, she's already more suspect in the eyes of the locals," Shaefer spoke up.

"Precisement." Jorisse nodded. "The people of Munier are a very provincial, old-fashioned lot. They tend to distrust strangers. Even Parisians such as myself are less than welcome there. A foreign woman like Miss West is automatically cause for deep suspicion. And there are reports she's been mixed up in other deaths as well." He eyed them quizzically.

"As a witness! She had nothing to do with the deaths of her brother Anthony West or Rachel Florry."

"Nevertheless, Miss West is a woman with a most...colorful history, is she not?" Jorisse noted drily. "And that could go very badly for her at trial."

"That's ridiculous!" Mary protested. "That Harriet

could be convicted just because she's a woman from another country. Isn't it ridiculous?" She turned to Shaefer.

"Sadly no," he replied. "If there's one thing I've become very aware of in recent times, it is how much being a non-native of a place can be held against you. Especially in the countryside. Prejudice is truly an international phenomenon." There was a bit of an edge to his voice, and Mary was struck again at the fact that Shaefer's position in England was that of a Jewish exile fleeing the horrors of his homeland. For him, gross injustice was simply a fact of life.

"Still, there is no guarantee as yet that Miss West will even go to trial, much less be convicted," Jorisse hastened to assure them. "I understand the local procureur is still hesitant to draw up formal charges. A great deal will depend not only on public opinion but also whatever further facts can be found about Mademoiselle West in the days to come and whether she had motive."

"Not just facts about Harriet," Mary thought aloud. "But Bill Holbrook too. Whether he did in fact have a history of assaulting women or behaving violently when drunk. That would support Harriet's defense."

"Oui, but only if such a history could be found," Jorisse noted shrewdly. "That is, I am sure why Mademoiselle West hired your services. For while everyone knows what happened, the questions of why and how are still very much up in the air. What for instance was Mademoiselle doing on the rampart wall with Monsieur Holbrook to begin with?"

"How would that be relevant if he attacked her?" Mary objected.

"Perhaps not but it is something people will be asking," Shaefer interjected, and Jorisse nodded.

"Precisely! What was the exact relationship between Mademoiselle West and the deceased? How did their quarrel begin? These are all questions a jury will want answered, I can assure you." He nodded emphatically. "You can imagine, then, how impatient I am to speak to my client."

"Wait, you haven't even met Harriet in person yet?" Mary was incredulous.

"I was only engaged yesterday, by her English solicitors," he responded before he could be accused of professional negligence. "Moreover, I was specifically instructed to wait for your arrival. A whim, it seems, on the part of Mademoiselle." A twist of his lips suggested Jorisse had not approved of that particular order. "As it is, the three of us are to drive to Munier together, where we are to meet Mademoiselle West and thereupon take up her defense together."

Jorisse had a black Peugeot and a swarthy-looking chauffeur, Raoul, to transport them all to Munier. Since the Peugeot had seats for only four people, Mary chose to ride up front with Raoul to let Shaefer and Jorisse talk.

"By the way," Jorisse told them both. "You can speak freely in front of Raoul. He has worked for me for many years and is the soul of discretion." Raoul made no verbal answer, merely tilting his cap in response. "Also, Raoul is originally from that area himself. So we can trust him to find his way on the roads."

"A local guide could prove very useful," Shaefer agreed.

In the car, Jorisse and Shaefer engaged in pleasantries.

"You know, I have quite enjoyed reading about your career as a private investigator," Jorisse confided as Shaefer modestly demurred. "But one thing troubles me. I can certainly understand"—he coughed delicately—"your desire to leave Germany."

"Leave isn't the word I'd use," Shaefer corrected him. "Fled is the more accurate term!"

"But why London?" Jorisse wondered, though his real question was "Why not Paris?" For like all true children of the City of Light, it was inconceivable to Jorisse that anyone should choose to live anywhere else. Especially England with its horrible weather, rude people, indigestible food, and ugly tweed clothes.

"Why not London?" Mary spoke up defensively. "It's the greatest city in the world!"

This was an assertion so absurd Jorisse could not even dignify it with a response, but merely a question.

"You've never lived outside of England, have you?" Jorisse suggested, and Mary bristled as sharp words came to her mouth.

"There were several reasons I chose England," Shaefer cut in before an argument could begin. "For one, I am already fluent in English. I do not," he noted wryly, "speak French. At least not with any degree of fluency," he amended.

"That would be an obvious advantage for England or America then," Jorisse admitted. "Still, there are plenty of English speakers in Paris. And you could have always taken up French lessons!" he chided them. For in Jorisse's mind, no one's education could be considered truly complete without a thorough understanding of French. He would acknowledge that fluency in other languages could be beneficial as well. Why else had his schooling included lessons in such a coarse tongue as English? But there was no getting away from the fact

that French was clearly the most beautiful of all languages.

"Secondly," Shaefer continued, "I already had contacts with persons in Scotland Yard who helped me get a
passport and find investigative work. It is actually quite
difficult to get refugee status in France these days," he
noted with a touch of bite in his voice.

"We cannot take just everyone who wants to come
here," Jorisse responded with an equal amount of bite.
"We would be overrun! We have enough trouble with the
constant tourists as it is. That is the one disadvantage of
living in the most beautiful city in the world—everyone
else wants to live here too. But I have no doubt an excep-
tion could have been made for the likes of you."

"Perhaps." Shaefer didn't look convinced by
Jorisse's obvious attempt at flattery. "But finally, Britain
seemed the safer choice to flee to in these times."

"Britain? Safer than France?" This was as if someone declared a hut with a straw roof a sturdier dwelling
than a mansion of red bricks.

"I mean no offense to your country," Shaefer told
him, all the while of course aware he was giving offense
anyway no matter how much he attempted to soften it.
"But the political situation here has proven somewhat...volatile." He coughed delicately.

"We do go through a lot of changes in regimes," Jorisse conceded. "And radicals on the Left and Right are constantly making trouble. They always do. Everywhere. Don't you have your share of radicals in England?"

"We do," Mary admitted. "Oswald Mosley's a real bastard, all right. But his crowd aren't the ones running the show in England, thank god!"

"Nor are they running it here in France!" Jorisse countered.

"Not yet at any rate." Shaefer spoke quietly. "Still, my impression is that Britain is at present a more stable place to be. After all," he noted wryly, "there's a lot more ocean between them and Germany right now."

"Even if you were right and Britain is safer—and I don't think for one moment that it is," Jorisse argued. "But even if it were somehow safer, I don't think it would be worth it to be stuck among the British!" He shuddered. "Mon Dieu."

"I can hear you!" Mary spoke up with some indignation.

"And surely even you can't deny a great nation like France has a much better chance of defending itself against armies than a tiny island like England," Jorisse went on. "After all we have the Maginot Line. I don't see the British Isles making any great preparations like that for all of Churchill's bluster."

"It's true, I'm less than impressed with the current British regime," Shaefer allowed. "But nevertheless, I have grown increasingly fond of the country while I've been there." This mollified Mary, and she practically beamed as he announced, "As it happens, I've now made some great friendships among the British people." Shaefer gestured toward Mary. "And acquired a number of valuable professional contacts as well. In France, I'd have to start all over again from scratch."

"So, we won't be luring you to cross la Manche anytime soon then?"

"Only for this visit," Shaefer replied firmly.

"Then we will have to make the most of it." Jorisse's good humor had returned. "Look at these views!"

Indeed, it was a very scenic ride from Paris to Provence and had Mary been in any mood to appreciate scenery she would have quite enjoyed it. Alas, her concerns were all on Harriet, and the beauty of the surrounding countryside was quite lost on her. So eager was she to get to Munier that she was quite put out whenever they had to stop for gas or the toilet. Or worst of all, when Jorisse insisted on having a very late—and very long—lunch at a certain quaint inn and restaurant he had patronized before.

"Why couldn't we have just picked up some sandwiches to take with us?" Mary hissed at Shaefer as Jorisse amiably devoured a three-course meal accompanied by a bottle of wine. "We need to get to Munier!" She barely even touched her dish despite its fine aroma, unwittingly insulting the chef in the process.

"I'm afraid, Mary," Shaefer told her drily, "that the French lack the appreciation for timeliness and efficiency possessed by we Germans or even for that matter you English."

Having eaten and drunk so well, Jorisse happily fell asleep in the back seat of the car and began snoring. After a moment's reflection, Shaefer decided there was no point in depriving himself of rest and he covered his eyes with his hat to doze a while as well. It was only Mary—and of course Raoul—who remained conscious during the entire drive.

As they rode on mile after mile, the landscape became less and less developed and as they went further south, they saw more vineyards, olive trees, and even natural forests appear. Eventually, one began to see the silhouettes of the fearsome Alps in the distance. Mary looked out at the scenery and marveled at what a strange journey it was for her to be making at all. She, the daughter of a lowly seamstress who'd clawed her way into the Queens Institute to become a district nurse, was now riding in a luxury auto in France in the company of a world-famous detective. Some days, even she couldn't figure out how that had happened.

Despite Raoul's excellent driving—he was, Mary thought, much better at navigating the Peugeot than Shaefer ever was driving his Aeroford—they did suffer the occasional hiccup. They came to a point in the road where an entire herd of goats was situated. The goats made no attempt to get out of the way of the approaching Peugeot but stubbornly stayed on their chosen path. Honking the horn had no effect. Nor did Mary getting out of the car and trying to manually shoo the beasts away. If anything, the goats only became more obstinate, and Mary suspected them of laughing at her under their beards. Now, as someone who'd spent a lot of time in the English countryside, Mary had become used to having roadways blocked by cows, sheep, and even pigs. But at least with other livestock species, the inconvenience had been entirely unintentional on the part of the beasts themselves. Whereas Mary couldn't suppress the suspicion that the goats were, in fact, acting out of malice rather than ignorance. This, she concluded, was exactly why goats as a species were not to be trusted and were in fact synonymous with evil across the world.

"At this rate, we'll never get there before nightfall!" she fumed while considering whether throwing a few well-aimed stones might improve matters.

"What can be done?" Jorisse shrugged. "Les chèvres seront des chèvres!"

Mary was in no mood for this sort of Gallic philosophy and might have said something inappropriate had a man in peasant clothes with a very shaggy dog not fortuitously appeared. It appeared the man was the owner of les chèvres in question, for his dog ran into the herd and nipped a few hooves and the goats dispersed.

"Merci!" Jorisse thanked him graciously. The man just grunted and went on his way.

*

It was very late in the day when they reached Munier, and the sun was beginning to set. Still, even in the fading light, the view was a grand one. The village itself lay upon a good-sized hill, and its limestone walls and tumbled roofs appeared to be cut into the very landscape. The bell tower of the church stood silhouetted against the sunset colors of oranges, pinks, and lavender. All was the same as it had been for centuries upon centuries. At first glance, one would think oneself transported back to the time of the Crusades. Even Mary was momentarily moved. Away in the distance they could hear the bells peal as human figures traversed the streets in the distance. It was a moment that seemed designed to be immortalized on canvas at the Louvre—or at the very least a picture postcard.

"Welcome to Munier," Jorisse whispered.

The town of Munier was indeed an ancient one. There was a half-buried old cemetery that went back to the days of the Romans. Other crumbling stone foundations suggested prehistoric origins, though it was hard to tell. That is the problem with anything of prehistoric origin; no one bothered in those times to write anything down, which is why everyone to this day is still baffled by Stonehenge. Most of what currently stood in Munier dated back to the 1700s with two notable exceptions— the Gothic church, completed in 1286, and the town's walls and fortifications. The latter had been constructed over a thousand years before and been steadily strengthened since.

Now, when a town, however pretty, walls itself off on the top of a hill it is for one reason only: to keep invaders at bay. The land had been assailed by invading armies from Central Europe before the death of Christ, only for those invaders to be overthrown by the Roman Empire. Along the way of all the blood and ashes, a group of settlers decided to make themselves a home on the rise where they'd finally be able to sleep easy. Their struggles getting all that stone up the hill and building their walls so high had been legendary. But all involved declared it worth it to make such a well-protected stronghold. Munier had, over the centuries of its existence, earned a proud reputation for being completely impregnable to any army. During the Middle Ages, when the Germanic hordes overtook the rest of the Rhone Valley, Munier alone remained free and untouched, a symbol of Gallic resistance.

And yet in the late sixteenth century, the Catholic stronghold had, after years of besiegement by the Heretical Huguenots, finally surrendered due to lack of drinking water. For five years, Catholics had chafed under the rule of the Protestants as Catholic armies, at the expense of Rome, fought to retake the city. Eventually, the Protestants were cast out and promptly butchered to much local acclaim. Over three centuries later, the memory had been glossed over and Munier had gone back to proclaiming itself an "impenetrable stronghold." True, like everywhere else in France, they had been touched by the Revolution and overthrow of the Bourbons, but they had avoided any actual fighting in their streets, rather cordially agreeing to live by the rules of whichever regime was in power at any particular time. Royalists or Republicans—it was all the same to the people of Munier. Unlike religious divisions, political ones never inspired the same fire in the local population.

Over the past hundred and fifty years, there had thankfully been no major battles, and life devolved into a bucolic idyll revolving around yearly grape crops. The bloody battles of the Great War had not come to their territory, remaining away in the distance. They had, however, lost a number of sons who'd marched off to battle elsewhere. They had fought, killed, and, in many cases, died in service to a so-called greater cause none of them had really understood. Those who came home told a tale of unimaginable suffering and waste brought about by vainglorious politicians and generals all too eager to throw other people's lives away. Surely, people said, such a war must never happen again. France could not survive it.

After a period of mourning, Munier built a memorial to its dead sons in the town square. This memorial not only honored the fallen but served as a warning to all that it didn't pay for townsfolk and their families to get involved with affairs outside their home. The warning was heard and obeyed. Citizens of Munier rarely emigrated elsewhere. Why would they when life was so comfortable where they were? The town's steep walls and buttresses were as good at keeping people within as they were at keeping people out. It was a town that closed ranks against outsiders.

It was also a town that knew how to guard its secrets.

CHAPTER TWO

Visiting hours at the prison had long since ended, so their priority was finding food and shelter for the night. Raoul quickly ascertained directions to a weathered stone inn on the outer edge of town that looked like it might have hosted Charlemagne at one point. Parking the car meant moving a red bicycle in the yard out of the way. The proprietor was a gloomy-looking fellow by the name of Gaston who smelled heavily of garlic and wine and didn't speak a word of English. Or at least pretended not to, despite having received more than a few American and British guests over the years. This was not just stubborn Francophilia but quite practical as well. Once

American and British visitors realized they couldn't converse with the innkeeper they not only stopped trying to engage him in conversation but tended to ease up on any demands they'd otherwise have made of him. Of course, this didn't stop French persons from trying to order him around, but he had evolved other methods for dealing with his fellow countrymen. Gaston, like his father and grandfather who'd run the inn before him, knew the importance of conserving one's time and energy, otherwise greedy guests would have drained him of both the way a mosquito drains you of blood.

He booked them rooms and offered them keys with an air of great reluctance as if he were taking them in against his own better judgement. It soon became apparent they were the only guests at this inn at present, it being the off season for tourists. Any illusions Mary or Shaefer might have possessed as to France offering a warm retreat after England were quickly dashed; it was a cold night, and the inn was drafty. And as the wind outside began to howl, everyone instinctively huddled by the enormous stone fireplace.

"Do you think we could get a drink to warm us up?" Mary wondered, rubbing her hands close to the fire grate. "And maybe a bite to eat?"

Jorisse spoke some words in French to the old

man, who grimly shuffled off. He was gone for a long time. This was in fact one of Gaston's strategies when dealing with French-speaking guests. He would not deny them service outright but delivering it at a glacial pace discouraged people from asking for it too often.

"Do you think we should send out a search party?" Mary jested half in earnest, but just then Gaston reappeared, deciding he had let his guests cool their heels enough. Any longer and they might have bothered to trouble him in person about it, which he would not have! And to his credit, Gaston had in fact brought them a good spread. He carried a large wooden tray offering a collection of cold charcuterie, cheeses, and breads and put it on a low rustic oak table near the fire lined with wooden benches. There was also a pitcher of something called Vin Chaud which proved to be a hot, spiced wine.

Mary drank deeply and gratefully. It warmed her bones and settled the nerves after what had been a long and trying day. Since she'd scarcely eaten at lunch, she tore at the food like a starving dog with a bone. Her unexpectedly ravenous qualities startled Jorisse but were no surprise to Shaefer, who was well used to Mary's hearty appetites.

As they sat by the fire, inhaling the sweet scent of woodsmoke, the shadows and flames danced along the stone walls as if they were conducting a pantomime theater. The old proprietor began speaking with Raoul in hushed undertones.

"What are they saying?" Mary asked Jorisse.

"I confess I am not sure," he told her. "They are speaking Provençal."

"What?" This came from Mary and Shaefer both.

"Provençal is a sort of local dialect," Jorisse explained. "It was banned over a century ago, but it lingers. Mostly because the locals dislike being told what to do by Parisian bureaucrats. Another reason we are lucky to have Raoul with us."

"Good lord," Mary murmured. "It'll be a miracle if we can get any communication done around here at all! How can you have multiple languages in a single country?"

"Fairly easily going by the Scottish and Irish in your country," Shaefer pointed out drily. "And don't the Welsh have their own tongue as well? Really, there are so many different accents among your people, I don't know how you keep track of them all, much less understand each other!"

"Point taken," Mary conceded. "Though I hear it's even worse in America."

This linguistic discussion was cut short by Raoul

speaking urgently to Jorisse. The latter frowned in response.

"What's he saying?" Mary asked, examining Raoul's troubled visage.

"He said the locals think it was no coincidence that the same night the Englishwoman killed the American was when the mistral blew in."

"The mis-what?" Mary asked, and Shaefer looked equally confused.

"The northwest wind," Jorisse helpfully translated. "This is the time of year when it blows most fiercely in these parts." To punctuate his remark, a strong gale hit the roof, causing the tiles to clatter. "There's a great deal of folklore in these parts about the wind," he continued. "It blows as much as a hundred days a year and is said to be strong enough to rip the ears off a donkey! And being superstitious, the locals claim that it sometimes drives people to madness and even murder."

"Really?" Mary wondered, clenching her hands without being aware of the action.

"Oui," Jorisse confirmed. "In fact, Raoul was just suggesting we use the mistral for Mademoiselle West's defense. Claim the wind made her do it!" He chortled at the ridiculousness of the notion, but Mary didn't smile.

"Would it work?" she asked him bluntly.

"Of course not!" he snapped back in irritation. "The idea is absurd. Someone kills a man because of a high wind? Bah! The idea is pure bêtise."

Gaston asked something of Raoul, and they had a hurried exchange with much shaking of heads and grave looks.

"Expliqués-tu!" Jorisse commanded his chauffeur, and a rapid monologue sprang forth that caused the former's jaw to drop.

"What?"

"He says something about a curse." Jorisse looked incredulous, young Raoul somewhat sheepish, and the old man defiant, his arms crossed firmly before his chest.

"Curse?"

"A curse on the chateau itself. People say terrible things once happened there and evil still walks the land."

"Templiers." Raoul spoke to Mary directly, and the old man nodded.

"Knights Templars," Jorisse translated. "The estate on which the Chateau Dellaire sits at one point housed a Templar stronghold. But then King Philip IV had them all burned alive."

Mary flinched at this detail. She had always found

such tales particularly disturbing and as a child had been terrified when reading of "Bloody Mary."

"Supposedly," Jorisse continued his narration, "King Philip did this because the Templars were heretics who dabbled in black magic."

"Supposedly?" Mary queried.

"Philip owed the entire order enormous sums of money so by condemning them as sorcerers he freed himself from a great deal of debt."

"Convenient for him," Shaefer noted.

"Quite," Jorisse agreed. "Just as how when he arrested all the Jews, he confiscated their money before banishing them from France!"

"Sounds familiar." Shaefer spoke lightly, but Mary could sense the bitterness from within.

"Still, the Jews were lucky compared to the Templars."

"That would be a new one," Shaefer muttered. Jorisse didn't appear to hear him but simply continued his tale. "King Philip accused the Templars of all sorts of sins: blasphemy, worshipping false idols...even homosexuality! All blatant lies of course but when spoken by the king, they had power. King Philip had them all rounded up and arrested. Then they were tortured until they would confess to anything."

"Again familiar," Shaefer muttered.

"Once he had their confessions," Jorisse went on, "King Philip ordered their executions. Not even the intervention of Pope Clement himself was enough to save the Templars from their fate. Over fifty souls were offered up to the flames. They say the screams of those slain at the fortress echoed for miles throughout the land. As the last of the Templars burned, he purportedly cursed King Philip IV and the Pope to both die within the year. Which, oddly enough, they did. The Pope died but a month later. They say his body was left in a church overnight only for the church to catch fire and the body to burn to ashes!"

"And King Philip?" Mary whispered, finding herself mesmerized by Jorisse's tale.

"In November that same year, he suffered a stroke hunting and soon died. His three sons followed him on the throne, each for brief reigns. Within fifteen years, they were all dead, and Philip's whole lineage, the House of Capet, extinct on the male side." Jorisse smiled. "You can imagine what that did for legends of the so-called Templar curse! But all that remains now are the ruins." His lip twisted. "And supposedly a bunch of very bitter ghosts."

"But the young American died on the town walls,"

Shaefer noted sharply. "Not on the grounds of the chateau."

Jorisse sighed. "Yes, but you can't try mixing logic with this sort of thing. He was at the chateau, so the Knights cursed him there. Or they cursed Mademoiselle to go mad." He rubbed the back of his head in exasperation.

The old man spoke again and made the sign of the cross.

"He says that the curse came to Madame Dellaire's late husband," Jorisse explained. "That it was why he shot himself."

"Good lord!" Mary was taken aback.

"Mauvaise affaire, ça," Raoul contributed to the discussion at hand. "Très mal!"

"After he died, Madame went away for a long time. People around here think she might have been better never to have come back."

"I see." Shaefer looked thoughtful. "I think I would like to visit this cursed chateau in any event and speak with Madame Dellaire."

"I agree," Mary concurred. "Find out what she knows—or, rather, knew about Bill Holbrook." And, she thought, learn more about his relationship with Harriet. It was, she told herself, crucial to Harriet's case. Still, deep down she recognized she was also curious to know what her former lover had been up to and during the months they'd spent apart. Not that she could expect Harriet to have practiced abstinence. After all, Mary hadn't and ironically her "companion" had been a French girl! It wasn't jealousy behind her curiosity—well, not much. Rather, she was fervent to know whether in Mary's absence from her life, Harriet had decided she liked men again.

None of this could be voiced aloud. Not even to Shaefer, though he was one of the few people on earth who not only knew the true state of Mary's preferences but even more remarkably had no problem with it what-soever.

"A visit to Madame Dellaire can certainly be ar-ranged," Jorisse agreed amicably.

Gaston let out another litany, and Raoul began speaking urgently to Jorisse.

"He claims there've been a lot of tragic deaths at the chateau over the centuries. Though, that"—Jorisse nearly rolled his eyes—"could be said of any ancient house, really. He also claims strange things happen there even now."

"What sort of things?" Shaefer spoke up. Jorisse looked irritated.

"Oh, the usual foolishness. Strange sounds. Reports of seeing figures on the grounds in twilight. Claims of woodsmoke and fire when there shouldn't be any. Just the sort of idle gossip you can expect from rustiques." Jorisse's tone was dismissive, but Mary was suddenly struck by the timing. Today was October 31st. All Hallows' Eve. Just the previous day, which now seemed like a century ago, she had carved a turnip and made plans to celebrate the occasion. She didn't know if they even celebrated All Hallows' Eve here in France, but now she was in this ancient, drafty old building talking about curses and ghosts! It was certainly one way to mark the occasion.

"Interesting," Shaefer mused. "It seems the chateau in general is always a place of interest in this area. Can he tell us anything about the people there?"

This time when Jorisse began his questions, Gaston deigned to answer him directly in French. "Non." He shook his head firmly and garbled something else.

"He says he is just a simple innkeeper who has nothing to do with the fine people at the chateau. He also says he can tell us nothing about them whatsoever."

"Hogwash!" Mary objected. "Sorry, but in my experience, people in small towns like this always know everything about their neighbors. Especially innkeepers."

"Perhaps you're right, but he's not talking," Jorisse noted, and Mary sighed. Good lord, would everyone in this town be as reluctant to speak to outsiders as Gaston clearly was?

"We shall speak to everyone at the chateau ourselves. Everyone at least willing to speak to us," Jorisse declared. "In the meantime, I plan to retire to my room. It's been a long day for all of us, and we will need our rest." These wishes were conveyed to the old man who ferried them all to their rooms one by one along with their luggage. Mary took off only her outer clothes before flinging herself into her bed.

She opened her eyes to find it fully dawn. Clearly, she had slept longer than intended. She looked around the room with fresh eyes, having been too exhausted the previous night to take any note of her surroundings. In the full light of day, it was quite a charming room with whitewashed walls and high raftered ceiling. The furniture was old-fashioned but in good condition; it consisted of the bed, a small desk and chair, a tall wardrobe, and a small end table. There was a faded chintz rug on the floor, and on the bed lay a beautiful white quilted bedspread decorated in an intricate design of sunflowers and goldfinches. As a seamstress's daughter, Mary knew quality stitching when she saw it. She fingered the motif, wondering whose hands had crafted such a treasure. It was double layered and plump enough to withstand winter cold, and sturdy enough to last a good long time. Yet it retained a delicacy in appearance that was quite marvelous.

After a quick change and visit to a bathroom down the hall, she went downstairs, following the smell of coffee. Jorisse and Shaefer were seated at the same table as last night, a mountain of breads and pastries in front of them.

"From the local boulangerie," Jorisse explained. "Help yourself!" He didn't have to ask twice. Mary immediately dug into a flaky buttery croissant, so good it made her moan. A mug of coffee was quickly produced for her as well.

"There is good news and bad news," Shaefer told her.

"Bad news first," Mary decreed. "Get it out of the way."

"Because today is All Saints' Day and a holiday here in France, the local jail is closed to visitors. So is the courthouse and most other official institutions in town."

"God damn it!" Mary swore aloud and was about

to continue with more uncouth expressions when Shaefer cut in.

"But while we can't see Miss West today, Madame Dellaire has agreed to an interview at the chateau at ten thirty. And this morning, I thought you and I could inspect the crime scene for ourselves."

"Crime scene?" Mary's eyes narrowed, and she crossed her arms in belligerent fashion.

"Alleged crime scene?" Shaefer hastily corrected. "Place where Holbrook died?"

"I guess we should see it," Mary conceded.

"And I would like to join you as well," Jorisse added. "If I cannot interview my client today, I can at least familiarize myself with as much background on the case as possible."

"Where's Raoul?" Mary wondered.

Shaefer spoke up. "He has, on my instructions, set about touring the town to meet everyone and gather as much intelligence as possible. Given that he's from the region, I suspect people will speak far more freely to him than to any of us."

"Also a good idea, since none of us can speak to the townsfolk," Mary agreed. "Not even Jorisse!"

The advocate took offense at that. "Oh, I can speak to them all right," he argued. "They all speak French as well as the local dialect. They just sometimes choose not to do so. Especially in the presence of outsiders."

"All the more reason, then," Shaefer proclaimed. "It should be one of their own who questions them. Come! I am most anxious to see where everything took place."

"By the way," Mary addressed Jorisse. "Can you ask the innkeeper where he acquired the beautiful bedspread in my room?" If it were available in a local shop, she might just take one home.

"You mean the boutis?" Jorisse asked. He spoke to Gaston briefly in French and to Mary's shock the old man's eyes began to water as if he were on the verge of tears.

"He says all the quilts here were stitched by his late granddaughter," Jorisse translated with obvious reluctance. "She had a remarkable gift, he says. What happened to her?" he questioned a distraught Gaston.

The old man shook his head and mumbled a reply.

"She went away to Paris to find work almost two years ago and died last winter," Jorisse reported.

"Dear god, tell him I'm sorry." Mary instructed.

"Elle vous présente ses condoléances," Jorisse told Gaston.

"Merci," the latter replied. He shuffled off, either

to attend to his duties or to be alone with his grief. Mary regretted ever mentioning the bedspread, and it was with some relief they left the inn.

Walking through town, they saw the bakery, the butcher shop, the grocery, and the local hairdressing shop. It was, Mary had to admit, a remarkably pretty tableau. More so than any English village she'd ever seen, though she'd never say a thing aloud. For while English towns were always a medley of browns and grays, Munier was burnished in yellow ochre, coral, and rose stones, with ruby-red stucco roofs and bright shutters of blue, lavender, and green on every window. Homes were draped with ivy, grapevines, and even green beans. It was as if the whole place had been transported straight out of the pages of a fairy tale. The belfry was a warm honey-colored stone building with an elegant Gothic arch. And the smells from the boulangerie perfumed the air with the tantalizing promise of good things.

During daylight hours, there was quite a bit of street traffic, with all the local folk going about their shopping and other daily business. Said locals, though, were often interrupted in their daily routines by the sight of the out-of-towners in their midst. Clearly, word had already spread as to their identities and their reason for being there, and they were the object of much scrutiny. The range of expressions on people's faces went from icy disdain to outright hostility. "Étrangers" was a word frequently murmured in their presence.

"We're not welcome here," Mary noted uneasily to Shaefer.

"That is often the case for me," he observed. Jorisse said nothing, but his walk was as stiff as it was brisk as they approached the town square dominated by the mairie. Next door, a large boules court was set up where a busy game was already in progress. As they approached, Mary noticed at least three different men wearing red sashes from their belts.

"Is that a popular thing here in France?" she asked Jorisse.

"Not France. Provence. It is a symbol you are a good native son of the region and a true patriot," Jorisse explained.

"Ah, patriotism," Franz echoed ironically. "Always a good thing that!" When Jorisse gave him an odd look, he went on, "It was the most fervent 'patriots' of the Fatherland who sent me away in exile." Shaefer's mouth turned bitter.

"Ah," remarked Jorisse. "Lucky we don't have that sort of thing in France."

"Not yet," Shaefer murmured so softly it was nearly inaudible. Jorisse caught his comment anyway and was offended at the implication. Nazis triumphant in glorious France? Never! But he wisely decided to stick to the matter at hand rather than get bogged down in a pointless political argument.

"Is that a mulberry tree?" Shaefer noted with surprise, pointing at one arboreal specimen.

"Good eye," Jorisse told him approvingly. "There was a time long ago when this region was actually a center for the silk trade. But sadly, those days are long gone." He walked on a little further before stopping. "Now, here is where the Feast would have been held." He gestured around the quaint common area now cleared of all its former festive adornment. "As you can see, everyone had a clear view of the wall right up there." They walked over to the rampart area. A section of the ground had been freshly scrubbed until the stones were almost shiny.

"This must be where he fell," Shaefer intoned. "They wasted no time in cleaning the area up." He sounded disappointed.

"Surely that's a good thing?" Jorisse asked with surprise. He did not consider himself an especially squeamish soul, but he was fastidious and preferred not to have blood and brain matter on the pavement.

"I would have preferred to see the cri—the scene of the death fully intact." Shaefer sighed.

"It's true, he does," Mary confirmed.

"That's one disadvantage of being a private investigator instead of a policeman. I never get to be the first one called in to see the body anymore!" He gave his head a slight shake. "Now let us take a look at things from above."

To reach the rampart path, they had to climb a great number of narrow stone steps cracked and crumbled in many parts. Mary was glad she'd worn sensible walking shoes instead of heels while Jorisse had to pause a couple of times to catch his breath. When they finally reached the top, though, they were rewarded with a glorious view. The cool weather of autumn had brought a banquet of colors to the surrounding countryside. Bronze and orange vines, red cherry trees, and bright-yellow woodlands against a brilliant sapphire-blue sky. A large white building lay flat in the center of all this like a seashell just dropped into the earth. Presumably this was the famous chateau Harriet had been staying at. It was exactly the sort of landscape irresistible to Cezanne and Monet. The air itself had a crisp sweetness to it that was a welcome reprieve after the London smog.

"It's a lovely place to walk in the daytime," Mary opined, "but why do so at night?"

"I was thinking exactly the same thing." Shaefer nodded at her. "What drew them both up here to begin with at that hour?"

"Perhaps to get some air?" Jorisse frowned. "Though this would not be my first choice," he admitted. "Imagine if the damned mistral caught you up here!" He looked alarmed. "In fact, perhaps we should go back down now?"

"A moment longer," Shaefer bid. "A man and a woman come up here for a walk." He frowned. "How well lit is this area at night?"

"I do not know, but on the night of the Feast, there'd have been bonfires and lanterns everywhere," Jorisse answered. "And it was the night of the full moon as well, so visibility would have been quite good. Perhaps they came up to stargaze?" he speculated. "Or maybe just to get a view of the celebration from on high?"

"I could see that," Mary mused.

"Or perhaps they wanted to enjoy a little privacy," Jorisse added, a suggestive gleam in his eye. "They were both young and unmarried, after all. And I am sure it would not be the first time a pair of lovers walked this way."

Mary could see that as a possibility too, but it wasn't one she wanted to dwell on.

"That is also possible," Shaefer thought aloud. "But whatever their reasons for doing so, two walked up this way. Only one walked back down. But not on a night when anything they do might go unobserved. No, this takes place during a public celebration when the entire town is watching!"

"That's good for our side then," Mary piped up. "Obviously there was no premeditation, which supports Harriet's claim to self-defense."

"I plan to point that out in my opening argument," Jorisse chimed in, looking pleased.

"True." Shaefer rubbed his chin. "But it cuts both ways, doesn't it?"

"How?" Mary looked up sharply.

"If as Miss West said, Holbrook suddenly attacked her, why would he do so in such a public setting? Why not lure her somewhere more secluded first?"

"Because he was drunk. Or a madman. Or a drunken madman!" Mary snapped. "He acted on impulse without thought."

"Oui." Jorisse's brow furrowed. "But they might say the same about Mademoiselle West."

Mary's face turned red with outrage, but before

she could say anything inopportune, Shaefer cut in.

"He's right. Oh, you and I know Miss West is not prone to irrational acts of violence, but the local judiciary sadly is not as familiar with her as we. Remember, Mary, we have to think of this case the way outsiders will see it." He spoke as gently as possible. "We cannot let our personal feelings get in the way."

Mary took in a few deep breaths. "You're right," she admitted. "I'll try to be more...impartial about all this. It's just so hard knowing there's even a small chance Harriet might hang."

"We don't hang people in France!" Jorisse spoke with considerable umbrage. "We gave that up long, long ago. The guillotine is far more efficient."

Mary blanched.

"Yes, I think we can go down now," Shaefer hurriedly suggested. "We don't want to be late for our appointment with Madame Dellaire."

CHAPTER THREE

They returned to the inn to find Raoul ready with the car. He spoke to Jorisse in rapid French.

"What did he say?" Mary asked, her tone sharp. She had been in France barely twenty-four hours and already the language barrier was driving her to distraction. She felt a newfound respect for Shaefer who had to navigate a foreign country at all times. Lord knew he had far greater patience than her!

"He said he's been all through town. Everyone's talking about what happened at the Feast."

"Naturally they are." Mary tried to keep her voice calm. "But what else are they saying?"

"There's been a lot of speculation as to why the Englishwoman killed the American man. Most say a lovers' quarrel brought on by jealousy, but there are others who think it might have been drug related."

"Of course, they do," Mary grumbled. "People always assume the worst."

"They generally do when it involves someone being killed," Jorisse reminded Mary. "What?" he responded to her look. "I'm only speaking the truth. We have to consider how others will see it. The prosecution will try to cast Mademoiselle's actions in the worst possible light, and I must prepare for that if I am to defend her."

Mary seethed, but deep down she knew he was right and so held her tongue, though she nearly had to bite it off to do so.

Raoul let out another litany.

"He also says he's heard a lot about the chateau. And about Madame Dellaire." As he translated, Jorisse's mouth gave a twist.

"Elle n'est pas dynamique," Raoul spoke up.

"What's that mean?"

"It means this may be an interesting morning," Jorisse answered obliquely. Mary did not find this a particularly satisfying response, but it was clear she wasn't going to get anything more out of him just yet. Raoul spoke again, and Jorisse translated. "Madame Dellaire's husband passed away about eight years ago and she has no children. Though I understand there is a nephew who lives with her. A Maxim Dellaire. It is he who will inherit the chateau. Indeed, he takes on most of the charge of the estate already." Jorisse looked bemused. "He also said something about Madame Dellaire having a pet artist! Another transplanted Parisian."

"This will be an interesting morning then," Shaefer opined cheerfully as they all got into the car.

*

It wasn't an especially long ride, but it was a bumpy one, the road being in some places little more than crushed dirt. They passed through endless orchards, vines, and groves of olive trees. As they did so, Mary noticed something odd.

"The olive trees all seem to be bending in one direction." It was true; they all stood slightly slanted as if some giant hand had pressed against them. Raoul spoke to Jorisse.

"Raoul says the trees here all bend to the south, because of how hard the mistral hits them from the north."

"My oh my," Mary marveled. "What are those?" They passed by a grouping of primitive stone huts, all of them shaped like miniature beehives. There appeared to be no wood or even mortar used in their building. Rather it was as if the stones themselves sprouted out of the ground like fungi and they were there before the first human settlers had even arrived.

"Those are bories," Jorisse proclaimed. "They're quite common in the area. Peasants would clear the land of all the stones and build themselves these little structures to store tools. Or occasionally to store themselves in cases of sudden storms, plagues, and other threats."

"They look quite ancient." Mary thought again of Stonehenge.

"Oui—they appear to be as old as the hills. But most of them were built no earlier than the 1700s."

"Perhaps some of them were used as shelter during the Revolution," Mary speculated.

"I think most aristocrats at the time would have considered living in such places a worse fate than the guillotine itself," Shaefer opined.

"I think I agree with Monsieur Shaefer for a change." Jorisse sounded as if it pained him to do so. "And few people ever stay in a borie for more than a single night. Except once. Legend tells of a shepherd boy who found himself lost in a snowstorm. After two weeks, the family had given him up for dead only for a huntsman to stumble upon the boy—by then quite famished with hunger—in a borie. For weeks, he had burned scrap wood to keep warm and melted snow to quench his thirst. They say when he was rescued the boy became quite devout and later joined a monastery to spend the rest of his life in service to God."

"Suppose it's a better reason to join the Church than because you've got an uncle somewhere to gift you with a vicarage," Mary reflected.

They came to a rusted old farm cart in the middle of road missing its wheels whereupon Raoul made a sharp left. A few moments later, the chateau came into view. A beautiful building carved out of pale stone in the Italianate state architecture that was so popular in eighteenth century France. It was by no means the largest or grandest property in Provence, but it was certainly one of the most charming with its rose stucco roof and crisp white shutters. It was framed on either side with chestnut trees, and in front lay an ornate fountain. Its white stone rendered it visible for miles around, making it an unofficial landmark. Many a person who found themselves lost or confused in the woods would be able to find their way to safety by simply looking out for a glimpse of the chateau. It was, in its way, as much a foundation of stability in the area as the church spire in Munier.

Someone inside must have seen or heard them from the road for as Raoul pulled into the drive, the main doorway opened, and a man emerged. He was a tubby little man with a bald, egg-shaped head and over-sized mustache, dressed in the formal uniform of a butler or valet. Raoul stayed with the car and lit a cigarette as his passengers got out.

"You must be the advocate from Paris," the bald man addressed Jorisse first in a heavy accent while taking furtive looks at Mary and Shaefer with a mixture of skepticism and confusion. "Madame is expecting you."

Finally, a French person besides Jorisse who spoke English! But Mary had no time to question him. He led them inside to a small blue-and-white parlor. On a loveseat sat an old lady. She could not have been an inch higher than five feet and was so petite it was as if she had the bones of a bird. Yet her eyes were bright and sharp and she seemed to radiate a presence that filled the entire room. She wore a light-gray Chanel dress of deceptively simple design, of a wool pressed so fine it seemed to be made out of a cloud. She also wore a chain of real pearls and a ring with a diamond the size of a pigeon egg.

"Thank you, Armand. You can leave us now." The old lady's English was flawless, her accent barely perceptible. She added as an afterthought, "And fetch us some refreshments as well."

Armand gave a slight nod and left. Jorisse introduced himself first, then Shaefer and finally Mary. Upon hearing Mary's name, the old lady raised her eyebrows.

"So, you are the famous Mary Grey? Well, well, well." She studied Mary so intently it almost made her squirm. What did the old woman know about her? What could she know even? Surely Harriet would never have confided to this Frenchwoman the true state of their relationship. But then again, Madame Dellaire might be a good guesser. It wouldn't be the first time someone had sniffed out the true nature of her relationship with Harriet. Indeed, the last time it had happened it had played a large role in ending said relationship. Mary made herself take on as impassive an expression as possible, and finally Madame's gaze moved away from her and to the men. It was only then Mary felt she could truly breathe.

"Let us begin," Jorisse suggested, "with how you met Mademoiselle West and came to invite her here."

"It was in late August," Madame Dellaire replied. "Every summer I like to visit Cannes. I go there for the sun and the sea, of course, but also for the people." She smiled wanly. "It is a good life here at the chateau, but it is often a quiet one. You never meet anyone new, but in cities like Cannes and Paris, there is always something happening. I prefer Paris in the winter and Cannes in the summer. This year in Cannes, I met Harriet West. A most beautiful and charming young woman. It seemed like every man in town was trying to win her favor. She seemed to enjoy the attention as well." Mary could not help but flinch at that. "Quite the coquette she was!" Madame smiled at the thought. "Not so different from me, mind you, in the days before I was married. Still, I could see something was troubling her. Having heard about her brother's death in England, I thought it might be that. But as I got to know her, I sensed she'd had—" Madame Dellaire hesitated before delicately adding, "other disappointments as well. She was not eager to return to England anytime soon, so I suggested to her she come and visit here. The countryside is most beautiful in autumn, and I have more than enough room." She waved her hands around. "When I am not visiting elsewhere, I enjoy having people visit me here. And the young mademoiselle certainly livened up the place." She gave another fond smile. "Good to have a beautiful young woman under this roof again. It has been too long."

"And what about Monsieur Holbrook?" Jorisse questioned gently, and Madame's face grew sorrowful again.

"Bill Holbrook was actually a friend of Fronsac's before he was a friend of mine."

"Fronsac?" Shaefer wondered.

"Henri Fronsac, an artist. He used to live in Paris," Madame Dellaire explained, "but it was so frightfully expensive that he came down to live in the country."

"This is definitely a good place for landscape painting," Mary noted.

"Oui." Madame declared with evident pride, "Moreover, here in Provence we have the ochre mines."

This statement garnered blank stares from all three visitors much to Madame's obvious annoyance.

"Ochre!" she repeated. "It is essential for artists!"

"It is?" Shaefer looked confused.

"Mon Dieu!" She raised her eyes to the ceiling as if praying to God above for the patience to endure such ignorance. "It is used in the paint. Artists mix ochres to make how you say? Pigments, yes, paint pigments. Ochre," she told them haughtily, "makes for the best natural pigment to come out of the earth. And Provence has the very finest pigments to be found anywhere."

"Really? How impressive," Mary dutifully responded.

A suitably assuaged Madame Dellaire continued, "So of course for an artist like Fronsac, it is a miracle to be here in Provence where he has access to the raw materials to make his own masterpieces. He rents a little cottage from me on the property. I'd have been happy to let him stay in the chateau itself, but of course he needs his privacy for his art. Now, back in Paris he'd known Holbrook. Holbrook was a journalist, you know, for an American paper. A most clever young man. About a month or so ago, he wrote to Fronsac asking about local places where he could find cheap lodging so he could write a series of columns for his paper about the French countryside. Fronsac asked me, and I suggested Holbrook could simply come and stay at the chateau for a while."

"Quite generous of you," Mary noted.

"As I said, the place is enormous, and I can do with company." Madame Dellaire shrugged. "And Holbrook was a very clever and amiable young man. One determined to make as much of his stay in the country as he could. He made a point of touring as many vineyards as possible," she noted drily. "And my nephew Maxim was more than happy to help guide him. But it wasn't all drinking. They also visited the old ochre mines in the area and went to Laguiole for the knives."

"They what?" Mary thought she'd heard wrong.

"The village of Laguiole," Madame Dellaire told them. "It is famous for its good knives."

"And for their corkscrews," a male voice added. Standing in the frame of the door was a man sporting a bright-blue beret over chestnut hair and mauve pantaloons stained with fern moss and berry juice. "Indeed, I have purchased a Laguiole corkscrew myself. It is worth its weight in gold."

"This is Georges Fronsac." Madame Dellaire introduced them to a man in paint-spattered overalls with chestnut whiskers, carrying a large wicker basket. "How delightful! We were just speaking of you."

"Nothing good I hope," he teased. "Voilà! I picked some blackberries for the chef, and I thought I'd say hello to Madame too."

"Merci," Madame said. "The berries look wonderful." She pointed to the others in the room. "They are here because of Mademoiselle West," she explained, and Fronsac let out a whoosh of breath. "Jorisse is her advocate from Paris, and Mademoiselle Grey and Monsieur Shaefer are"—was it Mary's imagination or did Madame hesitate a moment before saying the next word—"ah, friends of hers from England. Though Monsieur Shaefer is originally German." Madame put grave emphasis on the word.

"Guilty as charged," Shaefer agreed with more than a hint of irony.

"Ah, a bad business that about Mademoiselle West," Fronsac declared solemnly. "To think of such a charming belle in prison! You know, I tried to convince her to sit for me once, but alas she refused." He sighed.

"Did you go to Laguiole with Holbrook and Harriet for the corkscrews?" Mary wondered.

"Non," Fronsac replied. "I already had my corkscrew. See?" He pulled the corkscrew out of his jacket pocket and proudly displayed the Laguiole label.

"You always carry it on you?" Shaefer asked.

"Here in these parts, you never know when you might need it. Now, I did join Monsieur Holbrook and Mademoiselle West on many of their other car trips so that I could get fresh views to paint. Except for the time they went hunting. I find it not to my taste no matter how much Maxim tries to tempt me. It is a shame to disappoint him," Fronsac sighed. "But sadly, I do not share his love of sport."

"Harriet didn't go hunting either," Madame Dellaire recalled. "She said she was a lousy shot and that she abhorred the sight of blood. Ironique, n'est-ce pas?"

"You say you met Miss West in August?" Shaefer interjected.

"Oui."

"And the two of you came here when?"

"At the beginning of September."

"But that was then two months ago! Quite a long visit," Shaefer noted.

"Not really," Madame demurred. "Provence is such a charming place this time of year and there is always so much to do. And as I said before, the young mademoiselle was in no hurry to return to England."

"And you didn't find it inconvenient? Having her here so long?" Shaefer continued, his gaze curious.

"Not at all!" Madame said with conviction. "I told you how good it was having all the young people around enjoying themselves."

"So, Bill, Maxim, and Harriet all got on then, did they?" Mary noted.

"Oui," Fronsac agreed. "Like the Three Musketeers, they were!"

"Which makes what happened all the more incomprehensible," Madame Dellaire observed unhappily. "Harriet was willing to brave Holbrook's driving, and he seemed happy to take her wherever she wanted to go. I think he was—how you say? Sweet on her? Most men were. Even my nephew Maxim." Her eyes twinkled. "Though I'm not sure if the mademoiselle cared a jot for any of them." Her tone was that of bemusement rather than censorship. "Not that she wasn't trying."

"Trying?" Jorisse looked baffled.

"I think she would have liked to have found love," Madame Dellaire declared. "But sadly, could not. At least not with any of her suitors here." She said the last words almost like an afterthought, and for a brief moment, her eyes met Mary's.

"Le compagnon qui a tout commencé." Again, Jorisse was confused. "Je ne comprends pas," he stammered.

"Peu importe." Madame waved a hand. "After all, Miss Grey wasn't even in France when the incident occurred, was she?" She smiled grimly.

"Is that what we're calling it?" Mary wondered aloud. "The incident?"

"What else would you call it? La poussée?"

"That means 'the push,'" Jorisse clarified. "My first question to you, Madame—"

"Did you see it?" Mary interrupted. "The push?"

"Not I!" Fronsac answered. "My gaze was elsewhere."

"I did," Madame Dellaire said simply. Two words

that conveyed so much. Mary's heart gripped in her chest. Shaefer and Jorisse both seemed stunned into silence.

"What did you see?" Mary clenched her hands.

"Harriet and Bill on the wall. Something was clearly wrong. There was an argument or struggle."

Ah, Mary thought, that would confirm Harriet's defense and her hopes began to rise only to fall again as Madame Dellaire continued to speak.

"But who started the argument or what the quarrel was about, I cannot say. Then Harriet pushed Bill. He fell. He died. Not right away though."

"He didn't?" Shaefer's tone was sharp.

"Non. Several people rushed to his side, and they saw him still breathing. It seemed he was trying to speak. But no one could understand him. Maybe because he was trying to speak English, or maybe because he was beyond the power of speech altogether. Who can say? It was complete chaos that night." Madame Dellaire's voice remained steady, yet her face became increasingly anxious as she recalled the terrible events, and Fronsac stepped closer to her as if to offer her his hand. "They called the doctor and put him on a stretcher to take him to the hospital, but then as they loaded him into the ambulance, he died. And that is when Constable

Giroux placed Harriet under arrest."

They were interrupted by the arrival of Armand with a silver platter filled with tiny porcelain cups decorated with gold leaf, a silver coffee pot, and cream server. Shaefer and Madame Dellaire both took their coffee black while Mary and Jorisse made themselves café au lait.

"How did Miss West behave the night of the incident?" Shaefer addressed Madame Dellaire.

"She was her usual self," Madame answered promptly. "Quite in good spirits I'd say, considering what an...eventful year it has been for her." Yep, thought Mary, "eventful" was one way to describe it. "After the push of course, it was different."

"Did she show contrition? Fear?" Jorisse inquired. "Did she display signs of a guilty conscience, or did she appear to be a woman who had a close call?"

Madame Dellaire thought carefully before answering. "I would say she was in a state of shock. Like she could not believe what had happened. That she had actually taken a human life even if unwittingly."

"So you do not believe Miss West to be a cold-blooded killer?" Shaefer concluded.

"No, I don't," she replied with conviction. "And if she'd truly wanted him dead, she could have found a much safer and less public way to do it." She sipped her coffee as if to emphasize her point.

"And you will testify to that?" Jorisse asked eagerly.

"I will." And Jorisse and Mary both let out involuntary sighs of relief. "But I also have trouble believing Bill Holbrook attacked her. The man was perfectly harmless!"

"Oui," Fronsac agreed. "Assez passif!"

"If Harriet says he did, then he did!" Mary retorted with more rancor than she intended. Jorisse looked askance, and Shaefer cleared his throat to try to signal to Mary she needed to calm herself. "She's no liar."

"Not in my experience she isn't." Madame Dellaire remained calm. "In fact, I consider her an unusually honest young lady for these times."

Mary wondered with amusement what Madame Dellaire meant by "these times." Did she consider modern young women more dishonest than girls from her day had been? Because Mary strongly suspected that was not the case.

"I had ample time to examine young Bill as well," the old woman continued. "He was not without faults; he had a fondness for drink and was in some ways what I would consider a weak man. But he was not a man of angry or violent disposition either."

"Sometimes they're not," Mary protested indignantly while the men in the room looked increasingly uncomfortable. "At least not publicly, until they get you alone. After all, he did go hunting with your nephew." As a general rule, Mary had a poor opinion of killing for sport. Oh, she understood wringing chickens' necks and the work of butchers. People must eat after all. She was even sympathetic to farmers' dispatching of vermin with rifles. But those were killings made of necessity not pleasure. She simply couldn't understand why some people delighted in the "thrill of the chase" and bragged about indulging their blood thirst. Trophy hunting struck her as ghoulish: making a display of the corpse of a once living thing! English foxhunters to her mind were a particularly specious lot.

"Sometimes, yes, that is true," Madame Dellaire agreed. "But again, I do not think it was the case for Bill. And he only went hunting to get an article out of it. And even if he were secretly a man bent on violence, it wasn't the most opportune moment for him, was it?" She didn't wait for an answer but kept speaking. "After all, he and Harriet were still in clear view of the entire crowd. All she would have to do is call for help."

"It might have been hard for anyone to hear her,

though," Mary argued. "Especially if it was windy that night."

Madame Dellaire seemed not to hear Mary but gazed at the wall. "I had to call his family you know. It was very unpleasant." Her expression was morose. "Having to tell them what had happened and that it might be some time before they could release the body and send it home to America. They want him buried near them, it seems, not on foreign soil."

Even Mary was silent at that. She'd become accustomed to thinking of Holbrook as at best an impediment to Harriet's freedom and at worst an ogre. It came as a shock to think he had loved ones who missed him. A little voice inside her head reminded her she wanted to think the worst of the deceased for Harriet's sake. "See?" the little voice whispered. "Shaefer is right. You're already letting your relationship with Harriet cloud your judgment." She naturally told the little voice to stuff it, and it did. For the time anyway.

Meanwhile, Madame Dellaire continued to speak. "I do not think either of them had evil in their hearts that night when they walked up those stairs. I saw only two friends stretching their legs and enjoying the view. But once they were up there something happened, and les choices ont mal tournée." She paused and took another sip of her coffee.

"Like what?" Jorisse whispered.

"I do not know." Her face collapsed into a mixture of exhaustion and sadness. "Perhaps it was the wind. Perhaps as Father Brunel would say le diable was up to his old tricks. There are only two people in the world who truly know what happened on the wall that night. And one of them will never speak again."

CHAPTER FOUR

For a long time no one spoke, but it was Shaefer who broke the silence. "Where is your nephew Maxim?" he inquired. "He spent time with Miss West and Holbrook. Perhaps he can shed some light on the situation."

"I doubt it," Madame Dellaire pronounced. "He has no more idea than I did how this could have happened."

"It is true," Fronsac cut in. "Maxim is quite ignorant of what could have caused this."

"Nevertheless, I should still like to speak with him," Shaefer replied.

"I as well," Jorisse agreed. "The more facts we can

learn the better."

"Very well." Madame rang a little bell, and Armand appeared once more while they exchanged a few words. "It seems Maxim is not inside," she told them. "Rather he is out on the estate grounds." She looked vaguely irritated to admit this. "Shall I summon him?"

"That won't be necessary," Shaefer replied. "We will go to him. I think we would all welcome a chance to see some more of this lovely estate."

"We would?" Jorisse looked suspicious.

"Of course we would!" Mary chimed in. "I could certainly use some exercise after all those pastries this morning."

And so it was that the three of them, with directions from Armand, set out on foot to find the elusive Maxim. Fronsac bid Madame Dellaire adieu as well and walked outside with them.

"In retrospect," Fronsac mused, "I found it somewhat strange that Holbrook and Maxim became friends. Maxim—he is very much a son of the soil for all his blood. He is wedded to the land. Holbrook"—and a note of distaste entered Fronsac's voice—"was something of a dilettante."

It was, Mary thought, an odd comment considering he had supposedly been Holbrook's friend.

"I am afraid I must now go. But I do wish you luck in representing Mademoiselle West," Fronsac told them sincerely with a tip of his beret. "She is a most charming young woman, and it would be une tragédie to see such a beauty go to the guillotine." On that morbid note, he left them, whistling a jaunty tune as he skipped away down the road.

"Rather a peculiar fellow," Jorisse opined.

"It seems Madame likes collecting interesting specimens for her chateau," Shaefer mused.

"She's probably lonely," Mary speculated. "Childless widow living in such a big empty house in the middle of nowhere."

"You speak as if she were to be pitied," Jorisse noted with surprise.

"Perhaps she is," Mary answered.

*

The hike to Maxim turned out to be far longer than Jorisse had anticipated.

"I don't know why this is necessary," he grumbled as his expensive leather shoes squished in the mud. "We could have summoned him to the chateau and done this over coffee like civilized people!"

"I like to see as much of everything as I can,"

Shaefer told him. "To better understand everything that happened."

"It's true, he does," Mary confirmed.

"But we already know what happened," Jorisse complained in plaintive tones. "And it didn't even happen here!"

Impeccable though Jorisse's logic may have been, Shaefer remained unmoved. Mary by this time was well used to her employer's idiosyncrasies to the point of not bothering to argue. Besides, she enjoyed the walk, chill and all. The smell of wet leaves was in the air as well as freshly crushed olives to be pressed into oil. Seen from up close, the underside of the olive trees had a silvery sheen to them like something out of an enchanted forest. It was not hard, Mary admitted to herself, to see why Harriet had extended her stay in the area so long. It was exactly the sort of place unhappy city dwellers dreamed of one day retiring to with a bunch of dogs and devoting themselves to "the good life."

They walked forever but saw no sign of the aristocratic future heir to the grand chateau. The only figure they came across was that of a lone peasant man hoeing deeply into the earth to dislodge an unwanted bramble.

"Where is he?" Jorisse fretted. He turned and shouted at the peasant, "Toi! As-tu vu Maxim Dellaire?"

"Je suis Maxime!" the man answered, and Jorisse flushed.

"He's Maxime," he told Mary and Shaefer unnecessarily. The man walked over to them, and Mary studied him with careful interest.

Maxim Dellaire was definitely not the sort of slender, debonair fop who came to mind when one pictured a Frenchman of privileged birth. Rather, standing before them was a muscular young fellow wearing overalls suitable for outdoor work. His face wore a deep tan suggesting long hours outside, and there was black earth under his fingers, probably from working with the hoe. Small wonder Jorisse had mistaken him for a tenant farmer. Yet Maxim also possessed an intelligent, sensitive face framed by curled hair the color of chestnuts.

"Hello," Shaefer cheerfully introduced himself, then Mary and Jorisse. "We came to find you," he explained.

"And now you have," Maxim noted wryly. "I'd offer to shake your hand but mine's a bit dirty." He wiped beads of sweat from his brow. "The war against the brambles here is never-ending."

"We didn't expect to see you gardening," Jorisse blurted out.

"If I am to inherit this estate this someday, should

I not understand it?" Maxim cocked an eyebrow. "Whatever Aunt Hortense may think, the days of the Bourbons, my friends, are long gone. A man must keep his eyes to his property if he wants to keep it. Besides, I like to work on the land. I find it soothes the mind in times of trouble."

"Which trouble do you mean?" Mary asked him directly. "The death of Bill Holbrook or the arrest of Harriet West?"

"Both," he told her. "I cannot make any sense of what has happened. It all seems like a bad dream." His mouth twisted into a grimace. "Perhaps the townsfolk are right, and an evil presence does linger here somewhere."

"You know about the rumors of a curse?" Shaefer queried.

"Everyone here knows. Aunt Hortense knows too, but she never speaks of it."

"Is there anywhere we can sit and talk?" Jorisse asked hopefully.

"Oui." Maxim led them through a grove of trees to find a small clearing with rustic wooden chairs. They sat stiffly as he led them through the events of the past few weeks since Holbrook had come to visit them. Of course, he had taken the American shopping in Laguiole! It had the best knives and corkscrews in the world. Just as Provence had the best wine and best fresh produce and really best of everything. He had found the journalist very amiable company, though in his opinion the man had been something of a dilettante.

"I know it is strange for a Frenchman to call an American a dilettante, but it was still the truth. For one thing, he did not believe in doing honest labor with his hands," he noted with disapproval. "A man whose so-called profession was writing." Maxim rolled his eyes. "And he was quite fond of the grapes, you know. Even by the standards we have here in France. A great one with the ladies too. I saw for myself in the local bars." He gave an ironic twist of the mouth, adding almost to himself, "That much he and Fronsac had in common."

"What about Holbrook and Harriet?" Mary tried to keep her tone casual without betraying how curious she truly was about the matter.

"He was interested in her but she not so much in him," Maxim opined. "Which, of course, made Bill all the more persistent."

"Do you think it possible he could have assaulted Harriet?" Mary asked, and Maxim frowned.

"I would not put it past Bill to make advances. But however...amorous he might have been, I cannot believe he would have tried to force himself on her. And surely advances alone are not worth pushing a man off a wall?" Maxim asked rhetorically.

"But she probably didn't mean to push him off the wall," Mary pointed out. "She might not have realized how hard she pushed at all."

"Perhaps." Maxim's expression was a brooding one. "No one can really know what was in her head that night. Perhaps she herself does not even truly know."

Good lord, Mary thought; matters were bad enough without going down the rabbit hole of existential theory!

"Was Bill Holbrook drunk the night of the Feast?" she asked him bluntly.

"Almost certainly. We all were! It is traditional at the Feast for every adult from the mayor to the laborers become aussi ivre que possible." For the first time, his face displayed signs of humor. "Fortify oneself for the winter!" Maxim pulled out a packet of cigarettes and offered them to the others; they declined. "Suit yourselves." And he lit one up.

"Ah." Jorisse grasped at this point. "An intoxicated man might well have shown a dark side!"

"But I'd seen Bill drunk before, and while he may have gotten a little belligerent about giving up his car keys, he was never violent." Maxim spoke firmly between puffs. "He couldn't even stand the sight of blood! And when I took him hunting and we killed our first sanglier—"

"Sorry, what's a san-gleer?" Mary interrupted.

"Pig. Wild pig." Jorisse mimed tusks.

"Like boars actually," Maxim clarified. "Big tusks!" He demonstrated with his hands on his face. "They are quite common here. Indeed, they rival the brambles in terms of their vexing. They eat every crop they can find, dig up fields with their snouts, and taunt our dogs every night. They are worse than locusts! Which is why it is so important to hunt them every year. Well, that and they taste good. But when I took aim at a giant male gorging itself on melons, Holbrook blanched. When I hit the boar twice in the chest he nearly fainted from the sight of blood." Maxim shook his head with disapproval.

"Really?" Shaefer's eyes narrowed in thought.

"Oui!" Maxim nodded. "I thought all Americans were cowboys but not Bill Holbrook. And when I told him it was traditional to take the sanglier's head for a trophy and that the brains were a delicacy he actually got sick in the bushes."

"My, my," Mary marveled aloud. Not so much at the late Mr. Holbrook's squeamishness as at the notion that pigs' brains would be considered a culinary treat. Then again this was a country famous for eating frogs' legs and snails.

"Afterwards, of course, he was very embarrassed. He made me promise not to tell anyone. I only speak now because he is dead, and it seems important to be truthful," Maxim told them gravely.

"We all appreciate it," Shaefer told him.

Jorisse nodded his agreement, adding, "Merci beaucoup."

Mary wasn't sure she shared that sentiment. It wasn't that she wanted the Dellaires to lie exactly, but so far, they weren't helping Harriet's case any. On the face of it, the whole matter seemed utterly inscrutable. Two people on seemingly amicable terms suddenly come to blows and one ends up dead! If only they could speak to Harriet to learn from her exactly what had taken place. For the thousandth time, she cursed the prison being closed to visitors just then. This thought was punctuated by the brief sound of gunfire. Jorisse started a bit.

"Pas de soucis!" Maxim reassured them. "Just other hunters in the area. Hopefully they take care to shoot game and not people."

"Have people been shot around here?" Shaefer asked seemingly out of nowhere.

"Oui," Maxim answered. "Accidents happen. Someone takes a shot at what they think is a sanglier only to find it is a man. It occurs more often than you might think, especially so when the victim in question is known to be on friendly terms with another man's wife." He snorted.

"Was Holbrook friends with anyone's wives?" This question from Shaefer evidently took both Maxim and Jorisse aback. Even Mary was surprised by it as well.

"Not that I know of," Maxim told him after a moment's thought. "But why would it matter? Unless you think Harriet pushed him out of jealousy perhaps?" The cigarette having been smoked down to a nub, Maxim threw it to the ground and snuffed it out with one of his thick green rubber boots scuffed by years of wear and tear.

"No, I don't think that," Shaefer said. "Tell me, was there anything at all odd about Bill or Harriet that night? Before she pushed him, I mean?"

"Bill was perhaps more out of it than usual," Maxim reflected. "I saw him stumble a bit. Another reason I am surprised he went up the wall. It is a dangerous place to walk at night even when sober." His face turned dark. "I never should have let either of them go up. But I was distracted with the dance." He sighed. "We all were."

Seemingly out of nowhere, Shaefer changed the subject, "Tell me, what do you think of Fronsac?"

"The painter?" Maxim blinked a bit. "A most excellent fellow!" He spoke with evident warmth. "Very fond of the outdoors and quite talented as a painter. Not," he admitted sheepishly, "that I am any great judge of art. Still, I quite like all the works he's shown me." He flushed, looking momentarily embarrassed. "He had me pose for him a couple of times as well for his sketches."

Of course, Fronsac had, Mary thought. If a painter were looking for a model subject for "Noble Rustic" he could not have found a better one than Maxim Dellaire.

"But Aunt Hortense thinks he has talent as well and she does know art," Maxim told them almost defensively. "That is why she gives him such easy terms on the rent."

"She certainly seems to like having company around since your uncle died," Mary said. "Practically running a hostel here, it seems!"

"Actually, she always liked having people about, but my uncle was by nature more solitary," Maxim explained. "He had no patience with having guests at all."

"Doesn't sound very social," Mary observed.

"Indeed, he was not," Maxim agreed. "He treated even my parents and myself like intruders, and my father was his only brother. We actually rented another cottage nearby so that my father could manage the land for his brother, yet the two of them could go days or even weeks without speaking."

"My, my," Shaefer muttered at this dismaying unfraternal behavior.

"My aunt was for a number of years quite starved for company. So when he died, the first thing she did after the funeral was invite me and my father to move into the chateau. Then she began having people come over as often as possible. Said the place needed human voices to drive away the ghosts." His mouth twisted. "Truth be told, I was always a little surprised she stayed here at all. So many bad memories! He shot himself, you know." Maxim lowered his voice with this final confidence even though there was no one else within earshot of them.

"Yes, we heard," Mary replied. "It sounds quite tragic."

"It was," Maxim agreed. "But not entirely unexpected. He was a very troubled man. Many of the Dellaires are." He smiled grimly. "Another thing we have to thank the Templars for, eh? Or maybe just our own cursed blood. At least my father died a natural death. Simple heart attack while walking the vineyards." As he spoke, the edge of a breeze began to blow, scattering pebbles in its wake. He turned back in the direction of the chateau.

"See there?" He pointed to a turreted tower on the left side of the building. "That was where it happened. He just walked in one night with a pistol and *bam*! My aunt found the body along with one of the maids. At the sight of him, she fainted right then and there. After the inquest, she had the room locked up. No one has stepped inside since. No one wants to either."

"An actual tower room that's now boarded up because of a curse?" Mary exclaimed. "Sorry, but it sounds like something from a Gothic romance."

"Not a romance," Maxim answered. "Very real! You can wash away the blood, but such a sin must leave its own mark, no?"

"Sin?" Shaefer inquired, raising his brow.

"But of course." Maxim seemed surprised such a thing needed explanation, even to a foreigner and a Jew. "Suicide is a mortal sin. An act against God himself and one that cannot be repented."

"Makes it sound worse than murder," Mary noted.

"To we Catholics, it is," he replied and even Jorisse gave a faint nod. "My aunt had to bury my uncle here on the land of the estate. She said it was because he loved the land so, but really it was because they would not let him be interred in the cemetery on consecrated ground."

For a moment, he was silent, gazing off into the distance. Then he shook himself as if to return his attention to matters of the present rather than shadows of the past.

"The wind has begun to turn," Maxim observed. "Soon the mistral will be in full force. We must get inside now, while we still can."

He was proven right. By the time they reached the chateau, they were faced with the kind of gale that frequently devours hats and lapdogs.

"Shall you come in and take lunch?" Maxim suggested. Jorisse eagerly opened his mouth to accept, but Shaefer spoke first.

"Thank you, but I am afraid we have pressing business back in town."

A disappointed Jorisse had to shout several times to get Raoul's attention to drive them back.

"Interesting young man," Shaefer reasoned when they were out of earshot of Maxim.

"Certainly not like any aristocrats or gentry I met in England," Mary agreed. "Far more of the earth."

"I suspect he's a rare type here in France too," Shaefer opined.

"What business do we have in town?" Jorisse

grumbled as they got into the car. "I am quite sure the hospitality at the chateau would have been excellent."

"Probably," Shaefer agreed absentmindedly, "but I am not sure we should accept it." Before explaining this odd comment, though, he segued to another topic. "Besides, isn't this the hour when your fellow Frenchmen will be sitting in cafés speaking over drinks?"

"Oui!" Jorisse answered as realization dawned on his face.

"Then that is where we must be," Shaefer reasoned.

"It's true we've done a lot of investigating in pubs," Mary admitted.

"Bah!" Jorisse looked disgusted. "English pubs are dreary places with wretched food and drink!"

Mary looked offended, but Shaefer privately agreed with Jorisse's assessment. Since emigrating from Germany, he'd experienced a marked decline in his dining options. Nor had he had a single good beer.

"Today," Jorisse enthused, "you will get something much better."

"Not pig's brains I hope," Mary spoke up. "Or frogs or snails!"

Jorisse stared daggers at her, and for a moment, they seemed to be on the cusp of an international incident.

"Raoul!" Shaefer spoke up loudly in intervention. "Do you know where we can get a bite?" Rather than wait for Jorisse to translate, Shaefer patted his stomach and mimed using cutlery. Raoul's face lit up with understanding.

"Oui oui!" He started the engine.

If they had thought the drive to the vineyard a rickety one, the drive back was doubly so. Mary wasn't sure if the mistral really could tear the ears off a donkey, but it was more than capable of blowing debris into the windshield to reduce visibility. It also seemed to make the nuts and bolts of the Peugeot rattle in a most disturbing fashion. At one point, a large tree branch flew past them at high speed, barely missing crashing into one of the back windows.

It was no less windy once they returned to the town of Munier. All the pedestrians who had been out earlier had now vanished from the streets. By the time they exited the vehicle, the bitter cold of the wind threatened to take the shirt off one's back.

"Where do we go?" Mary shouted to make herself heard, and Raoul gestured for everyone to follow him inside a red-painted door. It opened into a long and narrow room lined with stone, filled with wooden tables all of which appeared to be occupied. The café felt very warm and snug after the cold wind outside, and Mary relaxed a little. The space smelled of garlic, cigarette smoke, wine, and savory dishes being prepared some-where in back. Everyone at the tables had been chatting when they opened the door, but as they walked inside, there was complete silence, and it seemed a thousand eyes were upon them. They crept their way far back into the room, to find the last unoccupied table in the whole café. As they did their best to squeeze all four of them in together without bumping knees, the other café patrons began speaking once more.

"Excusez-moi, voulez-vous commander?" A lanky man with hair slicked back high from his forehead ad-dressed them.

"He wants to know what we'd like to order," Jorisse happily changed the subject.

"I'm not familiar with the menu," Mary com-mented.

"No matter." Jorisse spoke to the waiter briefly, and the latter immediately stepped away.

"What did you tell him?" Mary asked suspiciously.

"I just told him to bring us whatever the lunch spe-cial for the day was," Jorisse replied with an expression of perfect innocence before adding, "and something to wash it down with too."

"Like what to drink?" Mary's eyes narrowed.

"Doesn't matter, it won't be German beer," Shaefer muttered gloomily.

"Just a local favorite is all," Jorisse reassured them. "You'll quite like it," he enthused before yelling, "Merde!"

"What?" Mary exclaimed.

"Something just ran over my foot. Are there rats here?" Jorisse fretted.

"Not exactly," Mary chortled as the interloper came out from under their feet into full view. A black cat with a single white spot on its chest and two white front paws. It paid no mind to Jorisse's indignant expression but began grooming itself with the natural superiority of its species. Mary instinctively held out her hand to offer it a head-scratching but was coolly rebuffed with a swish of his tail.

"He's not anymore keen on outsiders than the two-legged locals are," she observed with a pang of regret. She missed her own orange fellow Ahab and felt a prick of conscience for having abandoned him. Again.

Raoul whispered something to Jorisse, and the latter gave a low whistle.

"What?" Mary asked.

"Apparently it is the mayor who just walked in. It seems he comes here often and always eats at a private table," Jorisse explained, gesturing to a portly, balding gentleman in the entryway, accompanied by a young lady of a distinctly piquant prettiness who dressed like she'd come straight from Paris. Her face was carefully made up, and she wore that shade of deep plum-red lipstick so popular for nightclub scenes in the movies.

"Is that his daughter?" Mary asked.

"Non," Jorisse answered. "His wife, Angelique. She is from Marseilles, and her father and Mayor Farigoule were old friends and business partners before his death."

"Ah," Mary noted as the server greeted the couple with servile obeisance before ushering them away to a private dining area. "Was she then part of the business contract?"

Mary spoke in jest, but Jorisse answered seriously.

"Probably. It is all very well and good, notions of marrying for a grand passion and such. But romance does not pay the bills in the real world. Madame Farigoule was left with very little after her father passed, and the mayor had been a widower for some years. Everyone considered it a most satisfactory arrangement."

Mary found herself wondering if Angelique

Farigoule herself would agree with that assessment. Trading in a bustling city like Marseilles for a middle-aged husband in the countryside would not be most young women's idea of a great bargain.

The waiter returned with a bottle and four glasses. Shots were poured for all, but it was an unfamiliar libation.

"What is this?" Mary wondered suspiciously.

"A local favorite, according to Raoul," Jorisse answered. Raoul spoke up again and made motions to drink. "He says it's best to just swallow it down as quickly as possible."

"What the hell?" Shaefer reasoned. "We are abroad. We might as well experiment."

They clinked their glasses together, then all took hearty swigs. It was like pouring molten steel directly down one's throat. It brought tears to the eyes, and for a moment, Jorisse, Mary, and Shaefer were united in a fit of sputters. Raoul, however, seemed unaffected as he poured himself another dose with gusto.

"I think we should get some water at this table," Mary finally choked out, and Jorisse did not argue but called out for a pitcher. Mary drained one glass, then another, and it did help her head a bit.

But the newcomers remained a source of

attention. Mary and Shaefer were by now used to being objects of curiosity in any new place they visited. They weren't, however, accustomed to such open hostility. At least Mary wasn't. Shaefer, alas, had experienced far worse in his own homeland.

A group of middle-aged women in particular gazed with disapproval at the whole group. But it was Mary who bristled. What was there about any of them to engender such scorn?

"Vers quoi le monde va-t-il se diriger? Une pute anglaise et une juive dînent parmi nous!" one of them sniffed as the others nodded. At that, Raoul's face blanched. "Vous vous attendez à une telle décadence à Paris pas ici!"

Raoul began to shrink inside his chair as if wishing to make himself invisible. Mary got the distinct sense that if he could he'd prefer to separate himself from the rest of the party altogether.

"What were those women saying?" she asked Jorisse.

"They've noticed you're not from around here." His eyes wouldn't meet hers.

"What are they actually saying? Precise words!" she demanded, and finally Jorisse told her. As he spelled out the language they had used, his eyes glued firmly to the tabletop the whole time, Mary felt her face grow red.

"If you'd prefer, Mary, we could always leave," Shaefer spoke gently while scanning the room.

"I'd rather not give them the satisfaction." She stuck out her chin, refusing to let these women hound them from the café. "Besides, I am hungry!"

"Hmmm," was his only answer. But his eyes remained troubled. Mercifully the waiter soon reappeared with a pot of cassoulet, and Mary made a point of digging in as heartily as possible to show the room how unaffected she was by her spite. In reality, she felt self-conscious during the entire meal and barely tasted her dish, though Jorisse and Raoul both proclaimed it to be excellent. It wasn't just outrage for herself and Shaefer that preoccupied her. The attitude of their fellow diners further exacerbated her fears for Harriet. Jorisse had warned her before things could go badly for a foreigner in a Provençal court, but it was only then Mary began to understand just how badly. What chance did Harriet have for a fair trial if people like this were to be her jurors?

Shaefer, too, mostly picked at his food. The whole experience was bringing back painful memories of his final years in Germany before he'd left. The French and Germans, for all their vast cultural divides and centuries of warfare, were at least unified in their mutual anti-Semitism. Indeed, hatred of Jews was often the only thing that bound the so-called Christian races together. Once again, he thought that what his people really needed was their own country.

Jorisse and Raoul at least both had good appetites, but even they found their enjoyment of the meal dampened. Jorisse was perturbed on two fronts; not only did it seem an unfavorable environment for his new client, but the behavior of the locals was giving a bad name to all French persons and in front of an Englishwoman and a German no less!

Meanwhile, Raoul wasn't sure how he felt being associated in the minds of other Provençals with persons like Parisian lawyers, odd English spinsters, and German-Jewish exiles. Thank god Munier wasn't his home village or he might never have borne the shame. Still, he suspected his prospects for socializing with any of the local jeunes dames were not good and that didn't help his mood either.

They were all secretly relieved to pay the bill and exit the place as quickly as dignity would allow. By mutual agreement, they returned to the inn where the mistral winds raged outside the door. Gaston brought out hot wine for all of them without being asked, and they eagerly quaffed it down.

"Still think the Nazis couldn't make any headway in France?" Shaefer asked Jorisse, his tone bitter. For a moment, the latter blanched, but he rallied.

"A few country yokels with the usual bigotry you find in small towns," he proclaimed haughtily. "But they are hardly representative of the rest of France. Remember, we elected a Jew—Leon Blum—as our president!"

"He's not president now, though, is he?" Shaefer challenged.

"No but he may well be again," Jorisse countered. "Personally, I do not wish it. Not because he is a Jew, but because he is a socialist. But for France to even put socialists in power shows whatever else our flaws, we are no friends to Fascist Germany. We are not perfect, but the days of the Dreyfus affair are now over."

"Tell that to Roger Salengro," Shaefer muttered darkly.

"I don't mean to interrupt your political debate," Mary said, "but we're here for Harriet, aren't we. And right now, I'm worried!"

"The good news is that as of yet we can find no evidence Mademoiselle West had any reason to willfully harm the deceased." Jorisse's mind had immediately switched back into attorney mode. "The bad news is we cannot find any evidence she didn't have one either."

"Of course not," Mary protested. "You can't prove a negative."

"Logically no," Jorisse demurred. "But sadly, court cases are not always won on the merits of pure logic."

Mary considered that. "You're right," she concluded with reluctance. "Our best shot at getting Harriet acquitted then is to prove that Holbrook did, in fact, attack her."

Shaefer cocked an eyebrow. "And how do you propose we do that?"

"By proving him a violent man."

"But from all accounts, he wasn't," Shaefer replied, and at Mary's indignant expression, he added, "You know I am on Harriet's side. But I am only pointing out what the prosecution will argue."

"Whether Monsieur Holbrook was truly violent or not," Jorisse announced, "I will certainly try to paint him as such. My strategy will be to put *him* on trial rather than Mademoiselle West. The blacker we paint his character, the better the odds are she will be acquitted."

Mary nodded her approval. "Get as much dirt on him as we can."

Shaefer winced. As a former policeman, he abhorred such tactics. Had it not been for his friendship with Mary, he might have dropped off the case right then and there, regardless of the promise of a fat fee.

"We must send inquiries to other places he lived in before he came to the chateau," Jorisse opined. "Even to America if necessary. The more we can find out about him the better."

"That I do agree with," Shaefer spoke up thoughtfully. "The more we know about all the players the better we will be able to understand what happened the night of the festival."

"But we already know what happened that night!" Jorisse objected.

"But we don't yet understand it," Shaefer countered. "No one here seems to."

Mary lifted her head defiantly as she spoke. "We'll find out tomorrow from Harriet."

CHAPTER FIVE

They did not venture into the village again, but rather that evening dined on a hearty pot of ratatouille offered by Gaston and washed down with a jug of rough red table wine. Conversation was stilted with everyone deep in the mire of their own thoughts, except for Raoul and Gaston who spoke freely—but only to each other. As the only two speakers of Occitan in the room, they effectively shut everyone else out. Eventually Raoul addressed Jorisse.

"He says he has a story for us," Jorisse told Mary and Shaefer. Truth be told, Mary was in no mood for storytelling, but it seemed churlish to say so and she agreed to hear them out. Jorisse narrated for them the tale he heard from Raoul that had come to him from Gaston.

"As you may know, Provence is famous for its truffles. They are literally worth their weight in gold, and a good truffle harvester can make a great deal of money. Sadly, truffles do not always grow on the property of the best harvesters—they are usually to be found on land that belongs to other people. Which is why truffle poaching has become something of an unofficial sport in the area."

"We have that in England too," Mary noted. "Not poaching for truffles but for grouse and rabbits. A never-ending war between gamekeepers and peasants."

"Oui, the battles can be quite fierce," Jorisse agreed, warming to his tale. "And one particular landowner not so far from here suspected his land was being trespassed on by just such a truffle poacher. One dark night, he lay in wait in the bushes with his shotgun. Just as he suspected, he heard a rustling off in the woods. He approached carefully and then surprised the intruders with his gun fully aimed. They consisted of a peasant, his wife, and the dog. The peasant's wife held a sack full of truffles stolen from the landowner. At least that is how the landowner saw it. The peasant and his wife tried to argue that if he couldn't find the truffles themselves it was only fair that they gather them but to no avail. The landowner was incensed. He pointed out that laws of precedence in the region meant he was entitled to shoot them both for violating his property. He demanded to know how much money the peasant had earned stealing the landowner's truffles. The peasant named a considerable sum.

"'Do you still have it?' the landowner asked him.

"'Oui,' the peasant answered. 'Hidden in a box under the floor of my cottage.'

"'Well then,' the landowner replied. 'Go get it and bring it to me. They were my truffles so it's my money. And just to make sure you return, you'll be leaving your wife with me.'

"Much to the wife's protestations, she was left behind with the landowner in the pantry of his house, while her husband and dog scattered off into the night to fetch the money. An hour passed and then another. There was no sign of the husband, and as night became dawn, it became clear he had no intention of returning. Indeed, he was never seen in the area again. He took the money and a few things and au revoir!" Jorisse snapped his fingers.

"So he just left his wife with an angry man with a gun?" Mary cried out. "My god, what happened to her?"

Jorisse addressed Raoul, and the latter shrugged as he spoke.

"He does not know," Jorisse answered. "The story does not say." Raoul continued speaking. "But he says the point of the story around here was that the land-owner's great mistake was in having the wife stay behind as collateral. Instead, he should have kept the dog."

"The dog?" Mary gaped.

"Oui. The dog. For a good truffle-hunting dog is of immeasurable value and the poacher would certainly have come back with the money for that. That, Raoul says, is the moral of the tale," Jorisse concluded.

There was a long silence.

"It's hard to believe such a story is actually true," Mary pronounced at length.

"Perhaps it is, perhaps it isn't, but that is not the point," Jorisse said. "After all, were any of Aesop's fables true or were they just lessons?"

And on that note, they all retired for the night.

*

The next morning dawned bright and chilly after a night of screaming winds. Mary was an Englishwoman, and inclement weather was the least of her concerns. It is always a delicate matter seeing a former lover for the first time since they jilted you. When this visit takes place in a prison to discuss how they came to end another human being's life, this is not something that is covered in any etiquette books. Her stomach felt as if a nest of hornets dwelled inside it and were now at war with one another. Much to Jorisse's bewilderment and Shaefer's concern, Mary rejected the morning's offerings from the boulangerie, and could only be persuaded to sip some coffee. Alas, coffee on an empty stomach only makes you additionally jittery, and Mary found herself tapping her foot enough to drill a hole into the floor waiting for the time they could leave for the prison. Even Gaston could see her anxiety and kindly offered her a morning apéritif to steady the nerves.

"Tell him no thanks since I have to keep my head clear this morning," Mary instructed Jorisse before adding, "but I might well need one after I get back!"

Jorisse did so, while Gaston shook his head sadly, reflecting on the foolish obstinacy of the English. But what after all could you expect from a race of people so backward they persisted in maintaining the pretense of a monarchy even in the twentieth century? Even the Germans had embraced modernity enough to rid themselves of the Kaiser.

The local jail was built directly into the sentry

walls of the town. It was nearly five hundred years old, dating back to a time when the town of Munier had been besieged by Protestants, who later themselves became besieged by Papists. It had thus been used as a place of containment and even torture for both sides of the famed War of Religion. It consisted of a few narrow stone stories that invariably heated up like an oven in the summer and were freezing cold in winter. It had the overall charm and ambience of the Chateau d'If, though none of the notoriety.

"Could have been worse," Shaefer noted.

"Can hardly be described as the Bastille," Jorisse agreed. "Or the Tower of London!"

"Hardly looks comfortable either," Mary noted grimly. Harriet was a pampered society girl used to the finer things in life. She could not find such an adjustment agreeable. And this was only a temporary jail cell. In the event of a prolonged trial, she'd probably be transferred to a larger facility where conditions would be much, much worse—and include female prisoners who were in fact genuine criminals. What chance would Harriet have in a place like that?

They entered through a black-painted door on the first floor to find themselves in a stone room whose only furniture consisted of a desk and a chair. In the chair sat a skinny figure in a gendarme's uniform. This person's face was not visible, for their head was buried solidly in a newspaper. He did not seem to hear their footsteps or make any sign of recognizing their existence.

"Bonjour!" Jorisse hailed him. The figure dropped the newspaper on the floor, revealing itself to be a thin anemic-looking young man with dark hair. He appeared scarcely old enough to shave. To Mary, he looked more like a bank clerk than a policeman, an impression furthered by how frightened he seemed to be of his unexpected visitors.

Mary had no way of knowing it, but in fact, the young policeman in question, Etienne Valmont, happened to share Mary's opinion that he'd have been better suited to working in a bank or other clerical office job than his present position. The chain of circumstances that had led him to his assume his current occupation of police officer had been through no choice of his own. His sole consolation was that at least in his present assignment at Munier there was little in the way of crime and certainly never any murders, so he didn't actually have to do much other than paperwork. Visitors—particularly strange visitors—always represented a threat that someone might be about to demand he do actual policing and he was thus very perturbed by the arrival of the newcomers.

He and Jorisse began a fast-paced conversation. Valmont seemed quite confused as to what if anything he should be doing and kept shaking his head.

"He keeps saying he needs to speak to his superior," Jorisse translated for Mary.

"And where is his superior?" she demanded.

"I do not know!" Valmont blurted out. "He said he had business elsewhere."

"You speak English?" Jorisse and Mary asked in unison.

"Oui—un petit peu! I mean a little," he stammered. "If you speak slow and clear I can understand."

"Well then." Mary crossed her arms, being careful to enunciate fully as she spoke. "See if you understand this. We are going to see the prisoner Harriet West and see her now!" She pushed her face up to his in a way that made the latter instinctively cower. "It was bad enough," she growled, "I couldn't come yesterday, but if you try to keep me from her today, I will shove you aside to go and find her. And if your superior has a problem with that, tell him to talk to me."

"Est-elle une felle?" the terrified gendarme squeaked out to Jorisse.

"Elle est Anglaise!" Jorisse gave his verdict.

"You better just take her to the prisoner," Shaefer spoke up gently. "I can assure you from personal experience, Miss Grey is not a woman to be deterred. Besides, surely Miss West should be allowed to see her attorney?"

Faced with an international assembly of French, English, and even a German person against him, poor beleaguered Etienne bowed to the inevitable. He fetched a selection of keys on a chain and led them up a narrow stairway to a padlocked door. It seemed an interminable wait as he struggled to find the right key, and it was all Mary could do not to rip the chain out of his hands and try herself. But eventually, he found it and the old door rusting on its hinges creaked open.

"Good lord!" a familiar voice called out. "What is it? Have you finally come—?"

Harriet was dressed in an ill-fitting women's uniform of material so coarse and unpleasant she normally wouldn't have used it for rags. Her hair was a mess, her eyes ringed with sleepless nights of worry. There was a furrow line above her brow. But in all important respects, she was still the strikingly beautiful woman who had broken Mary's heart but a few short months ago.

"Mary," Harriet whispered. "You came!" Her eyes met Mary's, and it was as if nothing else in the universe even existed. Nothing was said, yet it seemed so much passed between them.

"Ahem." Jorisse cleared his throat with evident embarrassment. "We have not yet been introduced. Mademoiselle West, I am your attorney!"

"Oh yes, of course," Harriet muttered, breaking her gaze away from Mary. The latter used the reprieve to do a quick scan of Harriet's current housing situation. The cell measured eight by five feet and the sole furnishings were a cot with a thin mattress, a rickety wooden chair, and a bedpan. The walls were plain stone, and the sole window was a tiny one located far above eye level with, of course, the prerequisite iron bars rusted with age. There were some old rust-colored stains on the ancient stone walls that Mary fervently hoped were caused by something—anything—other than blood.

Jorisse spoke hurriedly to young Etienne.

"He says we can use the interrogation room to talk."

The interrogation room was located in the back area of the first floor. It couldn't be called a cheery or comfortable space, but there was a table with enough room for Harriet and all three of her visitors to sit at. Etienne hovered at the door, unsure of what to do.

"Merci. You can keep watch outside the door," Jorisse suggested, aware of Etienne's obvious discomfort with the situation. This suggestion appealed to Etienne, yet still he lingered.

"But shouldn't the prisoner be wearing cuffs?" he wondered.

"Is that really necessary?" Shaefer responded. "Surely she is no immediate threat?"

"He's right," Harriet agreed. "No walls I can push anyone off in here! Sorry, poor time for jokes, I suppose." She smiled wanly. Etienne left.

"I need to hear the whole story from you, Mademoiselle, in your own words," Jorisse began.

"We all do!" Mary chimed in. "It's the only way we can make sense of any of this."

"But that's the thing," Harriet told them. "It doesn't make any sense to me either. And I lived it. I was there!" She sighed and ran her hand through her hair. "God, I'm gasping for a fag right now."

Mary pulled out a packet of cigarettes and a lighter from her handbag and passed them to Harriet without a word. She grasped both eagerly, but then paused.

"You don't smoke."

"They're for you," Mary replied. Another look passed between them.

"Your story, Mademoiselle?" Jorisse insisted, gesturing to his watch.

"Yes, of course." Harriet lit up and took a good long puff. "You know I've been staying with Madame Dellaire at the chateau, yes?"

"We know," Shaefer spoke up. "She told us how she invited you to stay." He paused hesitantly. "She also told us you'd been spending quite a lot of time with her nephew Maxim and with the victim. I mean with Bill Holbrook," he corrected himself.

"Yes," Harriet said between puffs. "Yes, I had."

"What was the nature of your relationship with the deceased?" Jorisse asked bluntly.

"You mean if we were lovers?" Harriet turned her gaze to her lawyer completely as if determined not to look at Mary just then.

"Yes," Jorisse answered. "Were you?"

"Yes. We were. Briefly anyway. A one-time thing only, you understand. Very casual on both our sides." She shrugged to convey how inconsequential it was.

"Can you provide more details?" Jorisse didn't look the least bit surprised. "I ask not out of prurience but to better know how things stood between the two of you."

"There's not much to tell. One night after a few drinks, Bill asked to walk me to my room. And I let him. I'd known for a while he was interested. So was Maxim, for that matter. And so that night, I let him join me in bed. On the understanding that he not read too much into it, of course. It was an...experiment of sorts on my part." Harriet's eyes grew furtive, and was it Mary's imagination or had the former made an involuntary gesture toward her?

"An experiment you say?" Jorisse wondered.

"To see if I liked it," Harriet answered obliquely. "Truth was, I didn't. I didn't dislike sleeping with him, you understand, but I didn't get any particular thrill from it either. The whole experience was rather a disappointment. Which is why when Bill suggested a repeat performance, I politely declined."

"And how did he take this rejection, Monsieur Holbrook?"

"Initially quite well. Perfect gentleman about it really. It wasn't like he was in love with me after all. In fact, that's why I slept with him instead of Maxim. I was afraid Maxim might fall in love with me, and I didn't want that." She finished the cigarette and threw it on the floor then squashed the butt with her foot.

"Très understandable," Jorisse agreed amiably. An Englishman hearing a woman say she wanted a physical relationship without emotional ties might have been shocked and indignant by such a confession. To a

Parisian like Jorisse, though, Harriet's philosophy seemed entirely sensible. "One would not wish to lead young Maxim Dellaire on!"

"Quite," Harriet said. "Though in retrospect, I think I was unfair to Maxim; I don't think he was ever in any danger of falling in love with me either," she declared airily.

"So even though you and Monsieur had been to bed together, you had no hard feelings toward him?" Jorisse queried. "No jealousy?"

"None at all." Harriet spoke with perfect sincerity. "And honestly, I don't think he had any either."

Mary's thoughts on all of this were a jumble. She decided she didn't mind Harriet having taken another lover—well, not much anyway. After all, she hadn't been abstinent during their separation either. It did bother her that Harriet, unlike Mary, had chosen intercourse with a man. But then again, the way Harriet described it, her fling with Holbrook had been a casual one. Indeed, Harriet had called it an "experiment." What sort of experiment? Mary had a thousand questions bursting inside her, but she dared not ask a single one. Not, at least, until she had the chance to speak to Harriet alone.

Assuming that chance ever came.

"And yet you say he became violent with you at the

festival?" Jorisse continued. If he had any notion of Mary's inner turmoil or any particular tension between her and his client, he was very careful not to show it.

"He did." Harriet's face clouded over.

"Tell us about it," Jorisse commanded.

"He was excited for the Feast. We all were. It had been all anybody in the area had been talking about for weeks. Maxim told us we shouldn't eat anything that day so we'd have a good appetite, and he was right. It was like a Roman feast and the wine never stopped coming. Bill especially liked that," Harriet noted wryly. "He's even fonder—was fonder of drinking than even I am, and you both know"—she gestured toward Mary and Shaefer—"I can throw them back pretty hard! Eventually we decided we could use some air, so we went walking."

"Whose idea was it to walk on the wall?" Jorisse asked.

Harriet thought for a moment.

"It's all a bit blurry, but I think it was Bill's. He said he was feeling a little woozy and needed some air. I figured I could do with some myself. And with a full moon out, it seemed like a good time to check out the view."

"At what point did he begin—" Jorisse coughed delicately. "—to make advances?"

"Advances?" Harriet shook her head in surprise.

"Never! It wasn't like that at all."

"But you say he attacked you!" Mary blurted out.

"And he did!" Harriet shot back. "But not that way. He wasn't trying to, you know, force himself on me."

"Then what was he trying to do?"

"I don't know," she uttered helplessly as her face contorted with the memory. "I don't know if even he knew."

"What do you mean?" Mary interjected.

"There was something wrong with him. Bill, I mean." She spoke in a voice so low as to almost be a whisper. "First, he said he thought he was feeling ill, so I suggested we go back down and find a place for him to rest. And then he just turned feral!"

"Feral?" Shaefer spoke up.

"Feral! Like a mad dog!" Harriet recalled. "His eyes were crazy, and he actually started foaming at the mouth. I got scared, and that's when he lunged at me. Like he was going for my throat. I got scared and pushed him. But I didn't mean to kill him! I swear on my life I didn't!" She raked her nails against her face in agitation hard enough to leave marks. "Can I get another ciga-rette?" she asked plaintively, and her request was imme-diately gratified.

She put the cigarette to her lips and lit it, then took

a long drag.

"Don't suppose I could get any pastis as well?" Harriet wondered half in jest and half seriously.

"Next time maybe." Mary gave a small smile. "I'll make sure to pick up a bottle first before coming here."

"Thanks." Harriet returned her smile gratefully. "God, I knew I should have stuck to my original plan and gone to Paris to see the Expo! There's this one painting in particular by this Spanish artist Pablo something or other that everyone's been talking about." She tugged her hair in frustration.

"Don't worry," Mary soothed her. "Once we've resolved all this foolishness and you've gone free, we—I mean you," she corrected, "can go to Paris and see all the paintings you like."

"Weren't you just there?" Harriet wondered. "What did you think?"

"For barely a few hours. We hardly had had time to take in the sights," Mary noted.

"Pity that," Harriet said sincerely. "If the two of you are in France anyway you really should see the City of Lights. Why, you've never been to the Louvre!"

"Getting off the topic of future travels, exciting though it may be," Jorisse broke in. "There is the matter, Mademoiselle West, of your trial first."

"Right." Harriet gave a sheepish shrug. "That."

"Now, if I understand you correctly," Jorisse enunciated carefully, "your defense is that Holbrook out of nowhere went mad and without any reason or provocation tried to throttle you?" His tone made it clear this was not to his mind a winning argument.

"I know how it sounds." Harriet's voice dripped desperation. "And I wouldn't believe me either. Even now I have trouble believing it. But it happened!" She appeared to be on the verge of tears, and it was all Mary could do not to take her in her arms. If not for Jorisse being in the room, she would have. A sudden thought struck her.

"You said Holbrook was foaming at the mouth. Do you mean literally?"

"Yes, actually." Harriet looked up with surprise. "Flecks were flying out of his lips like a dog with rabies."

"What are you saying? That he had rabies?" Jorisse sounded incredulous. "We are going with a defense of rabies?"

"Or possibly some sort of narcotic," Shaefer speculated.

"That's something!" Jorisse looked excited, grasping on to the possibility. "Could Holbrook have been under the influence of drugs? Had he used any before?"

Harriet considered for a moment.

"I think he mentioned trying absinthe in Paris once among other things. But he wasn't using anything here in Provence. Or at least I never saw him using anything here," she corrected.

"If he had ever used drugs, though, perhaps it drove him to a fit," Jorisse mused aloud. "A judge could believe that." For the first time during the entire interview, he felt a surge of optimism.

"I have seen violent behavior from persons under the influence of cocaine or opium," Shaefer agreed thoughtfully.

"And there are other things besides street drugs which could account for it," Mary proposed. "Epilepsy would account for foaming at the mouth and mental confusion. Had he any history of epilepsy?"

"I don't know," Harriet replied as something like hope entered her face. "But are you saying it could have been some sort of medical condition?"

"Very easily," Mary asserted. "Anything from head injury to fevers to bad mushrooms."

"We ate mushrooms that night!" Harriet piped up.

"Did you see anything unusual about them?" Mary asked, and Harriet struggled to think.

Their discussion was interrupted by the door

swinging wide open to reveal an unhappy-looking Etienne accompanied by a middle-aged balding fellow in uniform bearing a scowl that seemed permanently etched into his face. This clearly must be the infamous Inspector Bruno they had all heard so much about.

Unlike Etienne, Inspector Bruno was a policeman by design rather than happenstance. It had been his chosen calling his whole life. What better career could there be than one where you wore a proud uniform, carried around a baton, and had the authority to enforce law and order over all your fellow citizens? He had eagerly pursued a career in the gendarmerie of Lyon and had been zealous in his rise through the ranks. It had been a very proud day when he had been told he was to be an inspector. But inexplicably, he had been stuck in such a minor and quiet little posting where most of his calls involved the theft of poultry. To him, involvement in an actual murder case had been a golden opportunity for promotion—or at least an assignment somewhere more interesting. And he was not about to let some oily Parisian lawyer and other foreign lowlifes ruin it for him.

"Who dared let you in here without my permission?" he snarled as Etienne cowered behind him.

"Perhaps you should talk to me." Jorisse was happy to intervene, for altercations with angry policemen were something he was long accustomed to.

A long conversation ensued between the inspector and Jorisse. The latter argued he had the right to confer with his client. The former countered that while Jorisse might have that right, who were the other people since they weren't lawyers or even French? And by the way, why wasn't the prisoner in cuffs? Etienne should have known better. Well, the inspector should not be so harsh on young Etienne, Jorisse argued. Anyone could see this particular prisoner was no threat. Look at her—such a delicate young woman!

Inspector Bruno declared he could be the judge of who was or wasn't a threat. And the young woman in question wasn't too delicate to have pushed someone off a wall. Even Jorisse had to give Bruno points for that one and so he changed tactics. Very well, leaving aside the matter of the cuffs, weren't prisoners allocated visiting hours? Oui, but visits could not go on forever! How long exactly had they been with the prisoner? Well, Jorisse admitted, they hadn't kept track of time—there had been so many aspects of the case to discuss. But if they'd already discussed all aspects of the case, the inspector argued, what did they have to stay around here for? Very well, as it happened, there was someplace else they had to be anyway. Could the good inspector be so kind as to direct Jorisse to the office of the coroner? The good inspector would not. Well, if the inspector was going to be so rude, Jorisse would just find out another way. Au revoir!

The general gist of this conversation was conveyed to Mary and Shaefer who both would have liked to linger longer but grudgingly accepted it was time to go. Before leaving, Mary waited until Inspector Bruno's eyes were elsewhere before hastily passing the packet with the remaining cigarettes and lighter to Harriet with a wink.

They went out of the police station straight into the mistral blowing so strong, Jorisse and Shaefer clutched their hats in their hands lest they lose them, and Mary feared for the buttons on her blouse.

CHAPTER SIX

Once back at the inn, Gaston declared himself ignorant of all matters concerning pathologists or even official hospitals in the area. What was wrong with the local doctor after all? Just two winters ago he had personally nursed Gaston through a bad bout of bronchitis. Couldn't they take their troubles to him?

Upon having the concept of autopsies explained to him, Gaston proclaimed himself quite disgusted by the very idea. What kind of madman would pick apart the bodies of the dead? He wanted nothing to do with such a thing!

Raoul and Jorisse had to make several inquiries to

local people to learn which hospital Holbrook's body had been taken to.

"They were so suspicious of us for asking such a simple question!" Jorisse grumbled. "What do they think we're planning to do? Steal the body?"

"Eat it possibly," Shaefer morbidly suggested. "After all, we Jews suck the blood of children, don't we?"

"Have you heard the English expression 'chip on one's shoulder'?" Jorisse asked, his tone cordial.

"Have you heard the one about 'head in the sand'?" Shaefer shot back. "It applies to you and millions of your fellow countrymen!" Their back-and-forth might have devolved into an international incident had Mary not intervened.

"Didn't they already send your office an autopsy report?" she addressed Jorisse.

"Not necessarily. Not without a formal request at any rate. And for that matter, it has only been a matter of days since Mr. Holbrook's death. It's entirely possible his body hasn't been examined yet. I doubt he was a top priority. After all," Jorisse noted drily, "his cause of death was already known."

Given the ruggedness of the roads and the lack of clarity in their directions, it took them over an hour to reach the official state-run hospital. It was a very modern and very ugly building that resembled nothing so much as a large concrete slab. Clearly of newer construction, it was utterly discordant with the general beauty and charm of the surrounding area. Mary had noticed before that hospitals were always a neglected field for architects. It was as if considering the buildings' proximity to sickness and death, they didn't even try to create a harmonious environment. Mary had always considered this unfortunate. For while the basic purpose of hospitals and sanitoriums was by definition practical and serious, surely it would do no harm to try to make them somewhat pleasing to those persons working or recovering within them? Hospitals were just as essential as churches and city halls. Why then did they never get the same grandeur in design? Or at least comfortable furnishings?

Once inside, they were greeted with the inevitable hospital aroma of antiseptic mingled with sickness. It was, though, a well-staffed facility, Mary noted, with a veritable army of white-coated doctors and nurses in starched collars all briskly going about their business. A couple of questions brought them to an office with a plaque labeled "Dr. Aubert, Pathologiste." They entered to find a woman of about thirty-five years of age with an angular face and dark hair held back in a very strict bun seated at a desk of dark polished wood. She looked irritated at being interrupted by visitors. The desk was covered in various official looking papers, and the woman was going over them with a pen. In the corner of the room was a skeleton that Jorisse involuntarily flinched at, much to the woman's apparent disgust.

"Excuse us," Jorisse began politely. "We are looking for Doctor Aubert."

"I am she," the woman answered coolly. It was then Mary noticed a framed certificate on the wall. It was written in French, but the name "Jeanne-Marie Aubert" was quite clear. Mary studied her with careful interest. Rare as it was to find a woman doctor, it was even rarer to find one who specialized in pathology. From what Mary could see of the woman, she looked intelligent but quite severe. Someone who probably knew her profession inside and out but did not necessarily possess a great bedside manner. It was a type of personality all too common among surgeons. Mary did not have a problem with women doctors—in fact, she quite admired their fortitude—but she didn't like the cold, unfeeling physicians of either gender. She had never understood why such hard-hearted persons pursued a career in medicine to begin with.

"My apologies, doctor," Jorisse quickly recovered.

"We are here regarding the body of one William Holbrook. We were hoping to receive a copy of the results of the autopsy."

"And how would that be any business of yours?" Dr. Aubert demanded. Jorisse took the time to explain the situation. Dr. Aubert gave occasional "Hrumphs!" along the way but was otherwise silent until the end.

"As it happens," she told them, "I had scheduled the autopsy on that particular corpse for this very afternoon." She checked her watch. "In another thirty minutes in fact. Once I finish up all of this." She gestured to the paper pile with a scowl. "If you care to wait, you'd be welcome to join me during the procedure." She said this somewhat facetiously, clearly not expecting them to take her up on the offer.

In Dr. Jeanne-Marie Aubert's experience, the vast majority of people couldn't stay far enough away from autopsies or morgues. Which was exactly why she'd chosen her specialty: she preferred the company of the silent dead to the noisy (and invariably irritating) living. Dead patients never complained, never told lies, never talked down to you because of your gender, and never bored you with inane small talk. They simply lay still and let you plumb their secrets one by one. From the very start as a medical student, she had quickly realized that anatomical examinations of corpses were by far her favorite exercise and, going on the age-old maxim that you should do what you love, had chosen pathology as her specialty. Many had been shocked and horrified; even her own surgeon father who had supported her dreams of becoming a doctor in the first place considered her choice off-putting. But she had never wavered and remained resolute in her path. She considered her present posting her reward. It was not the largest or most prestigious of such laboratories in France, but it was hers. Her own little fiefdom which she defended quite fiercely. She knew many people considered her cold—even ruthless—and did not care. If they wanted someone to hold their hand, they should see a nurse not a pathologist.

"That won't be necessary," Jorisse queasily exclaimed at the same time Shaefer said, "Thank you! I would be delighted to sit in!"

"Well, which is it?" Dr. Aubert demanded. Jorisse and Shaefer shared a quick glance.

"I believe," Shaefer suggested, "that Monsieur Jorisse would like to be excused to go back to Munier and work on matters there, while I can stay behind to attend the autopsy."

"Correction," Mary added with a beaming smile, "while *we* attend the autopsy!"

Dr. Aubert was now already regretting her rash invitation. But in her defense, how could she have foreseen two foreign civilians being this interested?

"Are you sure?" Shaefer asked Mary with concern. He was a long regular attendant of autopsies, but he knew Mary, despite her medical background, had declined such visits in the past.

"Quite." Mary was firm. "The morgue's never been my favorite part of hospital work, but I can stomach it."

"Very well." Shaefer turned to Jorisse. "You can head back to town. When you get there, I suggest you and Raoul do some visiting. Try to find out as much as you can from the locals about the chateau and all of Madame Dellaire's guests. And her tenant the artist fellow too."

"Of course," Jorisse agreed, relieved he wasn't being asked to join the autopsy. "But how will you get back to the inn afterwards? There is no phone to call."

Shaefer turned to Dr. Aubert. "Is it possible to hire a driver around here?"

"Of course it is." She gave an indignant sniff. "This is France not Africa!"

"Then we should be fine," Shaefer proclaimed. Jorisse was more than happy to leave the dismal world of hospitals far behind without ever stepping foot in the morgue.

Dr. Aubert asked Mary and Shaefer to wait outside her office until she was ready. It was more like forty-five minutes than thirty. Shaefer passed the time with his default activity of staring into space brooding while Mary became increasingly fidgety. She would have killed for a newspaper or anything else to read, but sadly anything to be found in the hospital was inevitably in French. She cursed herself for not bringing a paperback along for the trip with her while examining posters on the walls made by the Ministère de la Santé Publique France. A large colorful tableau of a wholesome-looking family of six was emblazoned with the words "La Syphilis Est Curable!" Even Mary figured she got the gist of that one. Another one depicted a woman in a nurse's uniform at the seaside with a group of children in bathing clothes with the label ANTITUBERCULEUX. What, she wondered, was with the trend of juxtaposing picturesque scenes of domestic tranquility with warnings against horrific disease? What, after all, did syphilis have to do with happy families or tuberculosis with seaside holidays? Or was the utter lack of a link between the subject matter and the pictures the whole point? Did the posters' designers think that cheerful pictures would somehow make messages on the matter of germ theory more palatable to the general public?

Being in a hospital also reminded Mary how nursing had been her first occupation, and she felt a hint of nostalgia. It was not that she regretted her change in career. The work she did with Shaefer was far too interesting. But she did miss helping patients. Perhaps, she thought, she could do some private nursing part-time while continuing detective work. She doubted Shaefer would object.

Finally, after what seemed like an eternity, Dr. Aubert completed whatever else she had to attend to and came out of her office.

"Oh!" she murmured upon seeing them, as if getting an unpleasant surprise. "I'd almost forgotten you. You're still here." Her tone was moderately disapproving as if she were disappointed in the pair of them for not having taken the hint to leave. What, however, could you expect from foreigners?

"We are. And we can't wait to begin," Mary assured her sweetly.

The pathologist ground her teeth, but she led Mary and Shaefer down a narrow green hallway to a morgue. It was the first time Mary had ever been inside a French morgue. Disappointingly, it was exactly the same as every English morgue she'd ever witnessed. If you'd seen one morgue you really had seen them all. Always the antiseptic smells, always the cool temperature, always the metal shelves, always the uneasy silence.

In front of the metal shelves lay a figure on a table covered with a sheet; William Holbrook's body carefully laid out for dissection.

"Are you ready?" Dr. Aubert asked them both. They nodded, and she pulled back the sheet.

Despite himself, Shaefer couldn't help but wince. Bill Holbrook's body, while still nominally in one piece, did not look good. The impact was most noticeable on the back of the skull.

"If it gets to be too much for you," Dr. Aubert spoke up hopefully, "you can always leave."

"No," Mary proclaimed firmly, sharing a look of conviction with Shaefer. "We'll stay." They were both professionally accustomed to this sort of thing. And they'd both be damned to give this officious Frenchwoman the satisfaction of leaving.

"As you wish," Dr. Aubert answered in an ominous tone. In the spirit of such professionalism, Mary forced herself to examine the body with an objective medical eye and quickly noticed something.

"That scar on his collarbone—did he break it?"

Mary observed.

"True," Dr. Aubert begrudgingly conceded. "I already X-rayed him as a matter of protocol." She pulled out a file with slides for them to examine. "As you can see"—she pointed to visible fractures lines—"sometime in the last two years he injured his collarbone, shoulder, and broke several of his ribs. But those old injuries had healed long before he even came to Munier. They'd have played no role in his death. Now, as for the injuries he sustained during the fall, even the most preliminary analysis shows extensive damage to the spine. Even if he had somehow survived, he'd have been paralyzed for life. And probably brain damaged as well. Perhaps all for the good he didn't live, eh?" she asked, expecting no answer.

"Was he on any sort of narcotic or hallucinogen at the time of death?" Mary burst out with impatience. Aubert gave her a cool glance.

"As someone who informed me you had visited the morgue before, you should well know," she announced haughtily, "that it is still too early in the examination for me to tell. For that we have to go deeper." She smiled with grim satisfaction before pulling a scalpel off the table. Then, with the dexterity of a dancer performing a well-choreographed routine, she made the first incision.

It was a good thing the deceased was a perfect stranger to both Mary and Shaefer or they might never have summoned the fortitude for what followed.

Chapter Seven

"Nightshade poisoning!" Jorisse's eyes were wide as saucers when he heard the news. "Is Dr. Aubert sure?" He, Shaefer, and Mary were all seated around a table at the old inn over a pot of hot tea. Gaston and Raoul were playing cards at an adjacent table and so far, from Gaston's laments, it appeared the latter was winning.

"Quite positive," Shaefer confirmed. "An examination of the organs of the deceased showed unmistakable signs of atropine poisoning. Dr. Aubert was actually quite excited to see such a dramatic example." He recalled the gleeful look on the pathologist's face as she realized she had an actual poisoning on her hands. "She sent out samples to a nearby laboratory to confirm it. It may take a while to get the official results back, but Aubert seems quite convinced. And it does line up with everything else."

"Wait, wouldn't there have been some sort of taste?" Jorisse objected.

"It's true atropine has a bitter taste," Mary conceded. "But given all the different foods and drinks he had that night, he might not have paid particular attention if he tasted one foul thing on the menu. He'd just toss it aside and move on. Or it could have been served to him in something that already had a strong bitter flavor and would mask the presence of poison. Atropine is quite deadly even in a small amount, and it explains everything that happened to him that night. Why Holbrook started feeling woozy, his foaming at the mouth, even his sudden burst of aggression...all perfectly consistent with nightshade poisoning." Mary's tone grew excited.

"So, he was acting under the influence of another substance but poison rather than recreational narcotics," Shaefer concluded.

Mary went on, "He was already dying when Harriet pushed him off that wall. The impact of the fall hastened the process, but the fact is he was a dead man walking. Dr. Aubert's already called the police, and once the lab results come in, it will be an official report. The police will have to release Harriet now."

"No later than tomorrow. Not an activity Inspector Bruno will enjoy," Shaefer noted with bemusement.

"Bugger Bruno!" Mary cursed. "Harriet ought to be released right away!" This was still a bone of contention for her that had caused much grumbling both at the morgue and during the cab ride back to Munier.

"Perhaps but there are still formalities to be observed," Jorisse pointed out.

"Oh, what is it with this country and red tape?" Mary groaned.

"If you think France is bad, you would definitely not have liked Germany," Shaefer drily suggested. "Long before the Nazis took over, we had a proud Teutonic tradition of making people wade through oceans of paperwork!"

"The irritations of bureaucracies aside, it seems my client has never been in any real danger at all," Jorisse mused, almost wistful. It was a shame to think his part in such an intriguing case was in fact almost a redundant one. Not that he had any intention of slashing his usual fees because of it.

"She was not. At least not so long as a proper autopsy was conducted!" Shaefer amended. "Though I wonder if good Dr. Aubert would have even bothered to do so without prompting on our part?"

"Surely it would have been required of her!" Mary objected.

"Maybe." Shaefer's expression was curious. "Maybe. But I know from personal experience that when a case seems so straightforward as this, the police are not always eager to welcome any sort of conflicting evidence."

"True," Mary conceded. "But I don't think that would have stopped Aubert. Oh, she's not the kindest of women and I can't say I liked her, but she does strike me as quite professionally thorough."

"Well, in any event, we are all very happy for Mademoiselle West's sake," Jorisse cut in before adding with a rueful sigh. "Though I admit I would have preferred a more proactive role in securing her release. The matter is finished then. Tomorrow, I return to Paris."

"But the matter is not finished," Shaefer pointed out.

"What?" Jorisse and Mary both turned to him.

"Someone poisoned William Holbrook. Presumably during the festival but we still don't know who or why."

Mary was startled to hear Shaefer's words and a

bit chagrined. She had been so focused on securing Harriet's freedom she hadn't stopped to consider the fact that they now had an entirely separate murder investigation on their hands.

"Hmm." Jorisse raised an eyebrow. "While that is no doubt of great interest to a distinguished detective like yourself, it is not really relevant to me. I was hired to defend my client, and since my client has now been exonerated, my role here is done."

"But has Harriet really been exonerated?" Mary worried aloud.

"Whatever do you mean?" Jorisse asked her.

"Fact is, someone did poison Bill Holbrook. What if they think Harriet did it?"

"And then what? Became impatient it wasn't working quickly enough and pushed him off a wall?" Jorisse looked scornful but then frowned. "Actually, someone could argue that! But"—his features relaxed once more—"they'd never make it stick in court."

"Still, in any event, the gendarmes will now want to interrogate Miss West once more," Shaefer reasoned. "To find out if she can shed any light on who might have poisoned Holbrook. In fact, they will have to now conduct an entirely new inquiry from an entirely new angle."

"And with the trail already getting cold," Mary pointed out, "and the initial crime scene already swept away!"

"Moreover, belladonna grows naturally in both the Alps and Mediterranean areas right here in France. So, unlike industrial arsenic or some rare South American poison like curare, it would have been relatively easy to acquire. Nor would it be possible to trace the source of the nightshade either. I do not envy the police this investigation," Shaefer opined.

"Hogwash!" Mary retorted sharply.

"What's hogwash?" Jorisse was confused.

"Not envying the police a difficult investigation!" Mary admonished Shaefer. "Was there ever a more bald-faced lie on your part? There's nothing you love more than cases like that."

"True, it does pose an interesting intellectual problem," Shaefer admitted. "One that I fear Inspector Bruno is perhaps not up to on his own."

"Which is why you're going to see the whole thing through, aren't you?" Mary deduced. "Oh, it would help to fully clear Harriet's name too, but I know you. You just can't resist the challenge."

"And can you?" Shaefer countered.

"Not really," Mary confessed with a sigh. "I am

now curious."

"As inspiring as it is to me, to see your dedication to the art of investigation," Jorisse said drily, "it is not, strictly speaking, my professional area. Once Mademoiselle West is officially released, Raoul and I will have to bid you farewell. I have many other affairs in Paris."

"We understand," Shaefer replied, and Mary nodded, though she knew without a translator—and a driver on hand—the investigation would go more slowly. Just getting back to the inn from the hospital had cost them a small fortune in cab fees from a driver with poor hygiene and who constantly sipped from a flask. This had made for an anxious riding experience, particularly as the driver would have to take one hand off the steering wheel for swigs. It gave Mary a newfound appreciation not only for Raoul as a chauffeur but even for Shaefer. Whatever else her employer's deficiencies as a driver, he could at least be relied on to stay sober.

"But for tonight, I would be delighted to have you join me for dinner. Raoul informed me of a restaurant— not the one where we dined yesterday," Jorisse clarified, "some half hour's drive away that comes highly recommended. Shall we?"

Mary accepted quite eagerly. She'd had nothing to eat all day except a couple of rolls, and her stomach was threatening a full-scale mutiny. Shaefer was more reluctant. He couldn't help but fear a reception similar to the one he'd received the other day at the café. Much to his relief, when they arrived at the restaurant, they were taken to a private room to eat. From there on, Shaefer was able to enjoy the repast almost as joyously as his dining companions. French cuisine was a major improvement over the fare he typically had to swallow in English pubs. Indeed, it might even be an improvement over German food—not that he would ever say such a thing aloud, especially not to Jorisse!

After a final round of desserts and cocktails, they began awkwardly stumbling from the table and down the stairs.

"Isn't that Madame Dellaire and Fronsac?" Mary nudged Jorisse, pointing at one of the tables.

"It is!" he marveled. The artist and the chatelaine were engaged in a fervent conversation. Madame Dellaire looked up, and her eyes momentarily met Mary's. Was it the latter's imagination or did the former blanch for a moment or two? But then she gave an imperious wave, summoning their whole party to her table.

"Is it true?" she demanded of them once they reached her table. "Was Bill Holbrook poisoned?"

"How did you know?" Mary blurted out.

"So, it is true." Fronsac gravely shook his head. "Une sombre tournes des affaires!"

"The news had Inspector Bruno quite upset," Madame Dellaire declared.

"And the good inspector told you about it?" Shaefer inquired with evident disapproval.

"No!" Madame Dellaire looked offended. "Inspector Bruno and I do not speak socially. But he told the mayor, and the mayor naturally informed me."

"And now the whole province knows." Mary realized English or French, there was no quicker communication system than that of a small-town grapevine.

"It seems impossible though." Madame was very agitated. "Why on earth would anyone want to kill Bill Holbrook? He wasn't even from here."

"Very strange," Fronsac agreed. "He had not spent enough time here yet to quarrel with anyone. Perhaps it was an accident?"

"I doubt it," Shaefer responded. "People sometimes get bad mushrooms by mistake, but belladonna berries are almost never served accidentally."

"Belladonna!" exclaimed Fronsac with real excitement. "A classic poison. That is what Emperor Claudius and Augustus were both poisoned with. By their wives."

Madame Dellaire gave him a dirty look. "But it is

such an awful thing to consider," she told them sincerely. "It was bad enough to have Harriet charged with murder...but now to think there is a poisoner among us." She looked fearful as if reconsidering her decision to dine out.

"So you have no idea then who might have been responsible?" Shaefer asked.

"None at all!" Madame declared with full conviction. "Even now it seems completely preposterous."

"Oui," echoed Fronsac, "it is simply inconceivable." But a twitch in his eye belied his words.

"Adieu, then," Shaefer told them, and they all stepped away from the table.

"Did you see how Fronsac reacted?" Shaefer asked Mary once outside.

"He definitely suspects something."

"But something he cannot or will not say in front of Madame," Shaefer mused. "We must find a time to talk to him alone when he'll be more receptive."

"Oh, is this what detective work means?" Jorisse interrupted. "Just going around asking people a lot of questions?"

"Pretty much," Mary confirmed, and Shaefer nodded.

"Ah, they make it seem so much more exciting in

the movies," Jorisse sighed. "All those chase scenes and shootouts!" He mimed his hand like a gun going *bang*!

"Neither of us even has a gun." Shaefer shook his head in amusement. "Even when I was a policeman, I never actually got to use one." What he did not say but thought was that as luck would have it, he'd later been in far greater danger from other so-called state authorities in his country than from any criminal. It had had the effect of turning him off policing as a profession altogether. Though not off crime solving. Fortunately, the two activities were not synonymous with each other.

"Sorry to disappoint you," Mary added sympathetically. It was never fun to burst someone's bubble.

"Quite the contrary," Jorisse said. "I like this intellectual approach much better. It's far easier on one's blood pressure!"

"I suppose it is." Mary considered the matter, surprised by Jorisse's answer. "Except for the time I went head-to-head with an axe killer!" Jorisse let a whoosh of breath at that and looked excited, so before he could ask any more questions, Mary hastily added, "But that's a story for another time."

They drove back to the inn in silence and were met with a volley of questions by Gaston. It soon transpired that he too had now heard the true cause of Bill

Holbrook's death and was naturally concerned. Who could have done such a thing? Why? Did the police have any suspects yet? Jorisse tried his best to reassure the innkeeper with limited success.

Poor old fellow, Mary thought, looking at the lines of worry on his face. He'd spent a lifetime living in a peaceful community and now out of nowhere, all sorts of dark and violent deeds were taking place. She'd seen it happen before in other communities rocked by a sudden and sensational murder. People were faced with the terrifying reality that a killer lived amongst them. Someone they knew—maybe even someone they considered a friend—was capable of the worst crime imaginable. For so many people, it rattled the very foundations of their community. Their first instinct was to always blame an outsider like Harriet. But now they'd be forced to look to one of their own for the guilty party and suspicion would invariably infect them all. Until the true killer was found, things in Munier might get very ugly indeed.

"He blames the mistral of course," Jorisse translated for them. "He says whoever poisoned the American must have been driven mad by the coming wind." As if to punctuate that point, the old innkeeper immediately retired to his rooms, firmly announcing that if any of his guests needed anything else they could get it themselves.

"Perhaps they were," Mary opined as she listened to the fierce gale even then waging outside. "Or maybe just the coming of winter and the shorter days and longer nights. Shaefer, has anyone ever done a study on murder and the seasons? Or murder and the weather?"

"That I do not know," Shaefer admitted. "But I doubt it." He gave a morbid chuckle. "Rather unfortunate. People come up with all sorts of explanations for murder: economics, heredity, and so forth. Why not meteorological rationales as well? It makes as much sense as anything else."

Jorisse had been eyeing Mary and Shaefer with a puzzled expression, and he shook his head muttering, "Je suis entouré des fous."

*

Upon retiring to her room, Mary felt restless. For one thing, she now had a new murder case on her mind, which was always distracting, but there was also the question of Harriet.

She and Shaefer had crossed the Channel on a moment's notice for one purpose only. To secure Harriet's release. They had done so. But now what? What on earth was she going to say to Harriet in the morning? "Congratulations on dodging a murder charge. What have you been up to in the months since you abandoned me?"

All right, so maybe "abandoned" was too strong a word. Mary was a full-grown woman not a foundling babe. But the fact remained that it had been Harriet who had ended things between them. Harriet who had broken Mary's heart, then called on Mary in her time of need to come to her rescue. What exactly was Mary to make of all that? How should she feel now? What was Harriet feeling now? Did she have any regrets about leaving Mary? It was more than enough to keep a lady awake at night listening to the wind. For that matter, the mistral was enough to keep a woman up all night all by itself. It howled, it bellowed, it sang out dirges in the dark. How many people had spent sleepless nights under such a cacophony? No wonder the locals associated it with madness! What exactly was the precise relationship between homicide and insomnia? Had anyone ever thought to do a scientific study of the matter?

She must have fallen asleep at some point, for how else could she have found herself suddenly awakened? There was a new voice added to the sound of the wind; an unearthly shriek like someone being stabbed in the night. She ran to the sole window of her room and tore open the shutter only to cower in fear as a ghastly pair of yellow eyes stared out at her from the darkness. She got the impression of a sort of mouth screaming in fury at her but could not hear anything over the roar of the mistral. A bolt of lightning appeared somewhere in the sky, illuminating the shape staring out at her.

It was an owl. Of course, it bloody well was!

"Bugger off!" Mary roared in a mix of embarrassment and irritation. "Why do you and your kinfolk keep hunting me anyway? I'm not even in England anymore!"

The owl's sole response was another long shriek before flying off into the darkness. Mary shuffled back to bed still cursing and tried her best to return to sleep.

CHAPTER EIGHT

The mistral did not let up all night, and even when the rosy rings of dawn finally appeared, the wind continued on, ruthlessly drowning out the cries of any roosters in the area as well as carrying off rooftop weathervanes. It may well have been enough to drive a person to homicide—but that person would have by necessity had to kill someone already under their own roof, for who would be fool enough to brave the elements on a night like that? It was certainly hard to imagine any housebreaker or poacher—no matter how desperate or determined—plying their trade under such circumstances.

As it was, with no fresh murders or other violent

crimes on his slate to distract him and with the irritating report from Dr. Aubert on his table, Inspector Bruno realized he had no choice but to formally release the Englishwoman. He was not the least bit happy about the situation. He had gone from having everything wrapped up in a neat little package to an open homicide on the books. Nor was this some matter of a nobody's corpse found with his head smashed in an alleyway which might go unnoticed. Bill Holbrook was a foreigner and a newsman, which automatically made the matter noteworthy, and his murder had clearly been a premeditated one. One he, Bruno, had almost no chance of solving given the coldness of the trail. His crime scene was now long gone. The memories of witnesses were no longer fresh. Potential suspects and miscreants had had more than enough time to destroy evidence and get their stories straight. It was, in fact, exactly the sort of murder that is a policeman's worst nightmare.

With his dreams of promotion so cruelly dashed, Inspector Bruno needed targets to direct his poor temper at. He started with Harriet since she was still technically in custody. Had she poisoned Holbrook? Well, she would deny it, wouldn't she? If she hadn't done it, then who had? He didn't receive a single satisfactory answer to any of his questions. Indeed, the Englishwoman, once she understood the new line of questioning, went from relief and surprise to a state of bemusement over the whole matter.

"So, I'm not a killer, then," she pronounced, cradling her head in one hand. "Does that mean I'm free to go?"

"Oui," Bruno muttered between clenched teeth.

"Thank god!" Harriet breathed a silent prayer to the heavens. "May I never see the inside of this place again! No offense meant to you," she offered to Etienne in the corner with a friendly smile, and the young gendarme blushed. Bruno's already foul mood worsened.

"But do not feel free to leave the area!" he snarled. "I may have more questions for you!" he warned with a wag of the finger.

"Right, right," Harriet muttered absently. "Do you know where the other strangers who came to town are staying?"

Bruno pressed his arms against his chest, giving no answer, but Etienne blurted out, "At Gaston's inn. On Rue de Vert!"

"Merci!" Harriet beamed at him while Inspector Bruno scowled. "Au revoir!" she told them both with a cheerful wave of the hand.

And so, just as an exhausted-looking Gaston was

making coffee and while Raoul had been sent out for croissants, Harriet West arrived on the premises. She wore the same clothes she'd had on the night of the festival, by then quite disheveled, and her hair was a bird's nest. She'd had no breakfast that morning and was in need of a good hot bath. But her voice hailed out loud and clear as she walked in the main area.

"Bonjour, everyone! Anyone got a cigarette?"

*

A great many things happened in the following hour. Raoul, having returned from the boulangerie, was sent off to the chateau to retrieve Harriet's things. Having not had time to eat himself, he put some of the pastries in his pocket for the road. Harriet snagged the last empty room in the inn and promptly went upstairs to enjoy a hot bath and a proper bed. Jorisse, Mary, and Shaefer breakfasted together.

"I have to admit the pastries here are quite good," Shaefer declared appreciatively, rubbing his stomach. He privately considered them a major step up over the biscuits and scones to be found in England. In fact, the superiority of French patisserie was almost enough to make him reconsider his choice of London over Paris as a new home.

"Maybe too good." Mary sighed. "If I stay here much longer, my figure will go to hell! Anyway, I better go get Harriet some more cigarettes before she comes down or we'll all suffer."

"Let me accompany you," Jorisse offered, "in case the local shopkeeper doesn't speak English."

Mary gratefully accepted, thinking how much more difficult things in Munier would be once Jorisse and the car had left. A quick word with Gaston informed them the local drugstore was a good place to buy cigarettes, and he gave them directions on where to find it.

"I do hope she'll be ready to go before this afternoon," Jorisse fretted as they walked. "It will be such a long drive back to Paris. And if we are out too late at night, we might have to spend another night at some inn!" He shuddered at the thought.

"And you're determined to take her back to Paris?"

"But of course," Jorisse answered. "I can hardly leave my client stranded here, can I?"

"But are you so sure she'll want to leave?" Mary wondered.

"What possible reason could she have to stay?" Jorisse reasoned. "Especially now that the weather's turned."

Mary saw his point; even when the wind wasn't

blowing, the air was chill and damp. Hardly the sort of thing that English tourists were inspired to stay in France for. Besides, watching someone fall to their death in front of you, then being wrongfully accused of cold-blooded murder, was exactly the sort of thing that would put a girl off a place no matter how picturesque it might otherwise be. How else to explain Harriet's desire that all her things be immediately brought up from the chateau? Likely after she'd had some rest, she'd be off in the Peugeot for Paris and after that who knew where? A stay in some Italian palazzo? A skiing holiday in the Alps? Or maybe straight back to England and the apartment she'd once shared with Mary. Whatever her fancies, one thing was clear. Harriet had no intention of remaining in Munier—or near Mary. Probably a good thing really, Mary considered. After all, a quick departure on Harriet's part would save them from later having an awkward conversation alone together. At least that's what Mary tried to tell herself, but she couldn't quite believe it.

"I for one cannot leave soon enough," Jorisse avowed. "How I have missed my flat in Paris!" Truthfully, Mary felt rather the same way about her room in London. But even the allure of home could not make her leave in the middle of a case. Still, it would have been far more convenient to have a car at their disposal. Perhaps

Gaston would be willing to give her the loan of his bicycle for longer trips?

They found their way to a yellow building with a bright-red door labeled "Pharmacie." They stepped inside to find a narrow but long space covered from floor to ceiling with shelf after shelf of tinctures, pills, and jars of penny candy. The walls were scrupulously whitewashed without a mark on them, and the floor was polished white tile. What wasn't white was black. In complete contrast to everything else in Munier, it was as if the owner here was trying to avoid color at all costs. Everything was so gleamingly spotless you felt the need to shade your eyes. The shop appeared to be completely empty with no signs of human occupation at all.

"Bonjour!" Jorisse made a sincere attempt at a friendly greeting, though his voice seemed to echo on the walls, thereby defeating the effect.

"Anyone here?" Mary cried out.

"I am here." A voice came from right over Mary's shoulder, giving her a start. Stepping out from some seemingly invisible passage was a skeletal figure with skin the color of chalk and spectacles as thick as soda bottles. He wore a long white coat that made him blend into the walls.

"I am Monsieur Duval, the proprietor of this

shop." His English was perfect with barely a trace of accent. Though perhaps that was also due to the reedy quality of his voice that crinkled like dried paper. Between his appearance and speech, he gave the disquieting impression of exsanguination and embalmment. More an animated husk than a flesh and blood human. "You must be the Englishwoman staying at Gaston's." He gave Mary a long unblinking look as he carefully took all three of them in.

"I am," Mary pointed her chin up, looking him right in the eye. She refused to let Duval unsettle her. "I understand you sell cigarettes here?"

Without a word, he led them to a display of various tobacco products. "These are the ones you want." He handed Mary a carton of Harriet's favorite brand.

"But I didn't say!" Mary noted with surprise.

"They're the same brand the other Englishwoman always bought in here," he replied. "I assume you're buying for her?"

"I am, but how could you know I was?" Mary quizzed him. "I might have been buying for myself, and who's to say I smoke the same brand?"

"You have no nicotine stains on your hands or teeth, so you don't smoke yourself. Which meant you had to be buying for someone else."

"You're right—I don't smoke," Mary admitted. "But how could you know the someone else I was buying for was the other Englishwoman? I came to this village with three other people, after all."

Duval remained unflappable.

"He doesn't smoke either." He gestured to Jorisse. "As for the chauffeur, he was already here himself for his own cigarettes. And if it had been the German fellow you're with, you probably would have come in earlier. After all, you've been here several days. But you only came after the other Englishwoman was released from the jail today. I suspect she's quite desperate for cigarettes now after being held inside for a while. Prisoners always are."

"Bravo!" Jorisse broke in, then looked somewhat sheepish. "Sorry, but it was most impressive on his part."

"You're right, it was," Mary conceded as she gave Duval a careful look. "You must use your powers of observation on a lot of people around here. Being the town pharmacist and all."

"Perhaps." A glimmer of smile appeared on the pharmacist's thin pale lips. "In Paris, one always has an endless parade on the street to examine. Here," he noted wistfully, "there are far fewer people to study. But," he added with a twinkle in his eye, "that means you can study them all the more carefully for it. Human nature under a microscope as it were."

Aah, Mary thought with excitement. Here it was. One never-ending feature of villages and small towns everywhere was the presence of habitual observers of human nature. Or as others liked to call them, busybodies. Mary knew from long experience that such individuals were of incalculable value to private investigators, and she and Shaefer made frequent use of them. True, most of the time, these persons were women rather than men. But she was open-minded enough to accept a gender reversal in this instance. She looked on the cadaverous figure of the pharmacist with a newfound appreciation Jorisse found bewildering.

"Monsieur Duval!" she exclaimed, holding out her hand to be shaken. He did so with a look of faint surprise. His skin felt as dry as paper, but Mary was undeterred. "I think you and I are going to be great friends."

And so it was that Jorisse returned to the inn alone to bring Harriet West her cigarettes. As he walked the cobblestones, he saw the town priest on the far end of the street. Father Benedict made no verbal acknowledgement, but clutched his rosary and made the sign of the cross. Jorisse was definitely not in Paris anymore. And he did not like it.

CHAPTER NINE

It was nearly noon by the time Mary walked back to the inn. She noticed a conspicuous absence; the Peugeot was nowhere to be seen. Surely Raoul would have returned from the chateau by now. He, Jorisse, and Harriet must have already left, eager to get back on the road to Paris. Mary felt torn between feeling relieved not to have to risk a face-to-face confrontation with Harriet alone and anger at her former lover for going off without even having the courtesy to say goodbye. Or could it be that Harriet had feared being left alone with Mary just as much as she did? There was a thought. But without Harriet there in person, there was no way to resolve the question. Perhaps, Mary told herself, it was all for the best. She and Shaefer didn't need the further distraction of Mary's personal life during an investigation. No, clearly it was better that Harriet had left.

She stepped into the inn—and there were Harriet and Shaefer sitting at the old wooden table with a checkerboard in front of them. Shaefer appeared to be winning, while Harriet was mid cigarette with an ashtray by her side full of stubs. Dressed in a freshly cleaned Chanel frock and with her hair and makeup carefully done, Harriet looked far more her old self than she had behind bars.

"You're here!" Mary blurted out, and Harriet looked up.

"Don't sound so disappointed," she answered.

"No, it's just I thought Jorisse and Raoul had already left."

"They did. After Raoul brought me my suitcase, I dismissed them since after all I don't need legal representation anymore."

"But how will you get back to Paris without a car?"

"When I have to, I'm sure I can hire a ride somewhere to the train station," Harriet responded coolly. "But I think for now I ought to stay in Munier. In fact, the ever-so-diligent Inspector Bruno practically ordered me to, and who am I to disobey him?" The amount of sheer cheekiness Harriet put into those words could have filled a bathtub to the brim.

"Don't tell me he still considers you a suspect?" Mary was aghast.

"Oh, I think he does," Harriet answered grimly. "He pointed out that I could easily have been the one to poison Bill before luring him onto the wall and then, in a fit of impatience, pushing him."

"That's ridiculous!" Mary could not conceal her indignation.

"Maybe, but it's what Bruno believes," Harriet noted. "And a lot of other people might believe it too, nonsensical as it is. I'm out of prison but my name won't really be clear until the actual poisoner is found." She went on before Mary could raise any objections, "And it wasn't that I particularly want to be an investigator, but no one likes feeling left out. The fact is someone did poison Bill Holbrook and in doing so was responsible for making me push the poor man off a wall! I'd rather like to see that person caught. So, for now I'm staying."

It was a gallant little speech, but there was an uncertainty in her eyes as she watched Mary, as if she feared the latter's reaction. This, Mary thought, was really too much to endure; one of the reasons she and Harriet had parted ways was Harriet's disapproval of

Mary's ambitions to join Shaefer as an apprentice. For Harriet to now want to play detective herself took considerable nerve and there was no telling what sort of inappropriate comment Mary might have made had she not been interrupted by the sound of Shaefer loudly clearing his throat.

"I am sure," he said, "that Miss West's presence will be of great assistance to us in this matter." Mary gave him a glare as he went on. "After all, she is fluent in French and has had more time to get to know the area than we have."

"It certainly would be useful to have someone familiar with the town who could serve as translator," Mary noted sweetly. "But as it happens, I've just come from meeting that someone."

"You have?" Shaefer looked surprised, and Harriet exclaimed, "Who?"

"The town pharmacist, Monsieur Duval," Mary answered them both. "He's been ever so helpful."

"Duval?" Harriet wrinkled her nose in distaste. "That anemic? I've always found him quite off-putting really. Like someone you'd expect to find haunting the local cemetery."

"Quite possibly," Mary agreed. "He certainly seems the type to go digging for bodies. But that's exactly why he's useful. He keeps his eyes and ears open to all sorts of dirty laundry all over town. And his English is perfect because his grandmother was from Jersey. So, while Shaefer and I appreciate your offer to help out, it really isn't necessary. You can hop off to Paris or wherever else you'd like to go. Enjoy some shopping!"

There was a long ugly silence with Mary and Harriet in a stare-off as Shaefer kept glancing warily from one to the other of them.

"Well, I'm not!" Harriet finally declared, folding her arms across her chest. "Contrary to what you might think, I'm not some spoiled rich girl with nothing but frivolity on my mind. Or at least," she corrected herself, "I'm not just that. I care about what happened here and I plan to stay a while." She jutted out her chin in defiance. "And there's nothing you can do to make me leave!"

The infuriating thing was Harriet was absolutely right. There wasn't anything Mary could do to make her leave. She looked to Shaefer for support, and he gave a shake of the head as if asking her what she expected him to do. He was a private investigator not an advice columnist for the lovelorn.

"Very well." Mary's tone was churlish. "You're a grown woman. Do as you like! But do you really mean to stay here rather than at the chateau?"

"It wouldn't have been my first choice," Harriet admitted. "But I'm not sure it's wise to go back to the chateau right now. I'd risk sharing quarters with a poisoner."

Mary's eyebrows rose. "So, you suspect Madame and Maxim Dellaire then?"

"I don't know," Harriet admitted. "I can't see any reason for them to do it. But the fact is they were at the feast that night, and besides me, the Dellaires and Fronsac were the people who spent the most time with Bill. Doesn't that make all of them the logical ones to look at first?"

"All right, now you do sound like a detective," Mary conceded.

"How much do you know about your hosts and their artist tenant?" Shaefer asked.

"I'll tell you everything over lunch," Harriet offered. "I'm still half-starved after that stay in jail."

Neither Shaefer nor Mary were pleased about returning to the local café, but Harriet soothed their feelings by getting them a private room.

"I'm still not sure I trust them not to poison my food," Shaefer grumbled.

"Now, now," Mary reminded him, "it was the other

diners who were behaving so awfully the other day. Not the people who work here." Even so, she thought that Munier, however beautiful it might be and however good the food, was not a place she'd want to stay in had it not been the scene of a sensational poisoning. As the old saw went, the problem with France was all the French people. Not that she had any illusions that her home country was free from bigotry. Mosley and his legion of followers were a vicious bunch whose influence Shaefer rightfully deplored, and Mary could legally be institutionalized for her same-sex tendencies. Nevertheless, England for all its sins still seemed safer than France, if only because Mary was more familiar with it. Though, of course, if Mary had grown up in France as Marie, she'd probably have considered France more secure than England. The devil you know isn't always better, but it always somehow seems better.

They received some less than hospitable looks as they walked in the café, but this time they at least had the relief of being quickly ushered upstairs for privacy.

"Is this where the mayor and his wife usually dine?" Mary asked their server—a different one from last time. This one was a young girl of no more than eighteen with dusky skin and eyes the color of licked chocolate bonbons.

"Oui, mademoiselle." She kept her gaze demurely at the floor, but Mary caught her taking the occasional glimpse of their dining party. She at least did not seem hostile but merely curious. "The mayor he is quite fond of the food here. He has dined in this café since he was a boy—as did his father before him."

"It's been around a long time, this café?"

"Oui," the girl said with evident pride. "It was founded by my great-great grandfather!" Then her mood became one of brisk business. "Now tell me—what would you like to order?"

"You pick," Harriet suggested. Mary wasn't so sure this was a wise course of action in a country where people regularly consumed frogs and snails but didn't know how to raise an objection without seeming rude. Shaefer was of the opinion that whatever culinary devilry the French could cook up could never be as bad as what the English served at mealtimes, so he was content. He did, however, have one instruction.

"Serve water only. Or maybe lemonade," he instructed the girl. "But no wine."

"No wine?" She could not have been more shocked if he had suddenly produced a chicken from a sack and cut off its head in front of them. More so, really. Like any girl in the country, she'd seen many chickens done in, but not even the local priest refused the nectar of grapes.

"No." Shaefer shook his head firmly. "It is very important that everyone at this table keep a clear head."

"So, no beer either then?" Mary spoke facetiously, and Shaefer gave her a reproachful glance.

"Anyway, it was a stroke of luck meeting Duval," Mary confided after their server had departed. She recounted how Duvall had known who Mary was buying the cigarettes for.

"Not bad," Shaefer agreed. "Perhaps it was he who should have become a policeman rather than Bruno or Etienne."

"Maybe," Mary agreed. "He also had a lot of interesting things to tell me about Mayor Farigoule and his wife Angelique. It seems the mayor's first marriage was a childless one. Everyone assumed the fault lay with his wife whose health was never very good." She paused.

"I can hear the but coming," Harriet noted.

"But so far, he's had no luck getting his new young wife pregnant either. It's been a grave disappointment to him that's made him consult numerous doctors to no avail. Though Angelique does not seem as upset. In fact, Duvall thinks she might be secretly relieved. The word is that she only married him to escape destitution after her father's death and is neither happy in her marriage nor about being out in the countryside instead of a proper city like Marseilles or Paris.

"For much of the village, the guessing game is not a matter of if she'll take a lover but when and who. So everyone took considerable interest when Fronsac asked her to sit for him as a model. She declined—apparently because her husband wouldn't let her do it."

"A jealous man, then?" Shaefer mused. "That's unusual among the French." At that point, they were interrupted by the return of their server bringing them a carafe of water and several glasses. She poured them all a glass with an expression of pity mingled with suspicion.

"Are you sure you don't want wine?" the server inquired plaintively. Harriet looked like she might order something, liquor being another luxury denied her in jail, but before she could speak, Shaefer did.

"No. We are quite fine with just water. Merci!"

The girl went away again, and Shaefer ignored the dirty look Harriet gave him. Only after she was sure the server was out of hearing range did Mary resume her tale.

"Apparently, the mayor wants to rest assured that any children Angelique does bear will be truly Farigoule's. It is the opinion of Duval and others that it's a losing battle on that one. And Angelique"—Mary led up to the note of true importance—"was once observed talking to Bill Holbrook. And he seemed to be quite animated in her presence."

"Wait—Bill and the mayor's wife?" Harriet looked incredulous. "That would be news to me!" She didn't appear jealous or perturbed in any way, merely surprised. Mary found herself pleased by this; clearly Harriet had not felt any particular romantic possessiveness toward Bill Holbrook even if she had bedded him.

"Duvall doesn't know for sure if there was anything more to it than a little conservation and attraction on Bill's part," Mary went on.

"That would be my guess," Harriet interjected. "It's not that I'd call Bill above having an affair with another man's wife. But I just don't see him with Angelique." She shook her head. "Nor do I think Bill would have been able to conceal such a thing from the rest of us at the chateau. He wasn't that good at intrigue," she noted drily.

"Even if you're right and nothing actually happened, there was gossip nonetheless," Mary pointed out.

"And older men can get very angry about handsome young fellows encroaching on their territory," Shaefer added. "I saw many such cases in Berlin."

"So we have to add the town mayor to our list of

suspects?" Harriet marveled. "That could complicate things."

"There's more too," Mary told them and waited until she had both their attention before spilling the next revelation. "They say back in the day, Mayor Farigoule was on very good terms with Madame Dellaire."

"What?" Harriet let out a shriek, then clasped her hands over her mouth.

Mary shook her head. "It's hard to be sure but the fact is Mayor Farigoule was married to an invalid and the late Monsieur Dellaire was from all accounts a very troubled man. If he'd been a poorer man or living in a city, he probably would have been locked away in a madhouse. As it was, they tried to keep him mostly locked up at the chateau. Madame Dellaire thus had a lot of free time, and she and Farigoule became, and I quote, 'the best of friends.' So naturally there was a lot of speculation as to whether they might be anything more. The general consensus is people think they were lovers at least at one point. But since they were both careful to be discreet about it, public opinion forgave them."

"How very French!" Shaefer opined.

"When they both lost their spouses, there were a fair number of folks who thought the two of them might marry. Indeed, Duval thinks they probably would have...had the mayor not been so anxious for a son to carry on his name, and Madame was by then too old to give him one," Mary concluded. "Hence his haste to buy...I'm sorry, *marry* a much younger woman. Duvall also thinks that while Madame Dellaire was disappointed, she ultimately understood. After all, Napoleon divorced Josephine, the great love of his life, precisely for the same reason."

"How cold-blooded," Harriet thought aloud. "But Napoleon did at least get a son and heir off Archduchess Marie Louise. Farigoule hasn't gotten one from Angelique."

"Which is why there's considerable speculation to the effect that Mayor Farigoule may now regret the marriage since it's given him nothing," Mary explained. "At least if he'd married Madame Dellaire, he could have moved into the chateau."

The sound of the door opening quieted them all, as the girl returned with an array of dishes. Mary did not recognize any of what she was being served, but it all smelled so good and she felt so hungry she couldn't help but taste it.

"Delicious!" She smacked her lips, eating a particularly divine buttery dish. "What is it?"

"Escargot," Harriet told her with a look of

amusement. "Namely, snails."

Mary paused a moment. Had she been informed beforehand she probably wouldn't have tried the dish, but now that she had, she had to admit it was quite good. And after all, were snails so very different from eels, which she'd frequently eaten in England? Both were slimy invertebrates after all, just one lived in dirt and the other in water. She happily helped herself to more dirt-living eels.

"I suppose I should have guessed about Madame Dellaire and the mayor. I knew they were old friends. He and his wife have visited the chateau. But somehow with older people you never think of them in that sort of way, do you?" Harriet mused.

"There may be more to the story as well," Mary added hesitantly.

"More how?"

"The fact is the late Monsieur Dellaire's death was quite convenient to his widow. And there was talk."

"Talk?" Harriet frowned. "What sort of talk?"

"There were some who questioned whether it was even a suicide at all," Mary explained.

"Wait, people suspected Madame Dellaire of having killed her own husband?"

"Some did. Others suggested Farigoule did it for

her. Or that the two of them did it together."

"But surely there must have been an investigation," Harriet objected, but Mary interrupted.

"Apparently the former police chief at that time was something of a crony of Farigoule's, which fueled speculation he might have agreed to hush the whole thing up."

"Dear god," Harriet whispered, visibly shaken. "I had no idea! What kind of people have I gotten myself mixed up with?"

"Again, mind you, it was all rumors. There was no actual evidence for any of it," Mary cautioned before Harriet let her imagination get away with her.

"And after all this time, it would be almost impossible to prove anything," Shaefer noted. "And even if it were true, how it would relate to the murder of Holbrook?"

"Unless he somehow found out," Harriet realized. "And threatened to tell."

"A possibility we cannot dismiss," Shaefer agreed. "But again unproven. Tell me, Mary, did you learn anything else from the loquacious Mr. Duval?"

"A few things. Fronsac the painter goes to Marseilles and Avignon quite a bit to sell to art dealers there. Maxim Dellaire buys up local farmland and property whenever it comes up on the market. He clearly means to expand the estate and is so busy with the land he doesn't seem to notice that half the girls in the county have their eyes set on him for a match, including the local schoolteacher, Louise Perrineau." What Mary did not add—could not add—was the speculation that Harriet was in fact the first woman to catch Maxim's eye.

"It's true," Harriet spoke up, "Maxim is a workaholic. Wedded to the soil and all. His aunt even worries about it. She's afraid he'll never get around to finding a bride and producing the next generation of Dellaires to run the chateau. It's why she was so keen to set me up with him."

"So, you knew she was trying to play matchmaker there?" Mary blurted out.

"Of course." Harriet seemed surprised it even needed to be said. "She wasn't exactly subtle about it. Practically been throwing the two of us at each other since I arrived." She rolled her eyes. "But contrary to whatever she may have told you, there's been nothing between Maxim and me." She spoke with conviction.

"So, Maxim would not have had any reason to be jealous of your tryst with Holbrook?" Shaefer spoke up.

"Good lord no!" Harriet seemed thoroughly surprised by the question. "I mean, I've never given him any reason to be. I never led him on. He's not holding some deadly torch for me whatever his aunt thought. It's all purely platonic, I assure you."

Harriet looked quite adamant, and it was clear she believed everything she said. But that didn't mean she was right, thought Mary. Maxim might have been harboring some secret passion for Harriet which could have motivated him to kill Holbrook. Or he might have had some grudge against Holbrook entirely unrelated to Harriet at all. Perhaps he'd been in love with Holbrook and had killed him out of pain of rejection.

Or for that matter, what about Maxim's aunt, Madame Dellaire? Had she really invited Bill Holbrook purely out of hospitality or had there been an ulterior motive? As improbable as it was, could the late Mr. Holbrook have had something on Madame and possibly been blackmailing her? A thorough check of the finances of the Dellaire family and of Bill Holbrook would have to be conducted. Mary was sure Shaefer would agree with her—had even perhaps already taken steps on the matter. She was reluctant, however, to broach the matter in front of Harriet. She had, after all, been a guest of the Dellaires for some time and might not be entirely impartial there. At least she was out of the chateau now and in the safety of the inn, Mary thought.

"And one other thing," Mary brought up carefully. "Duval had quite a bit to say about your dear friend Inspector Bruno."

"Oh?" Harriet cocked her head with interest. "Any secret vices we could use to blackmail him with?" She spoke as if it were but a jest, but there was a certain hunger in her words as well. Harriet had had quite a lot of Inspector Bruno's company over the last few days from her cell and would have welcomed anything to make him be the one to squirm for a change.

"It seems he's quite the hypochondriac. Always trying out new tonics and purported remedies for wellness. If anyone so much as coughs or sneezes in his direction, he reacts like they're pointing a gun in his face," Mary told them with a grin, and Harriet snorted with glee. "Thought you might get a laugh out of that."

"I do. But I'm still not sure Duval's entirely trustworthy. I mean, he was at the Feast himself. Had as much chance as anyone else to poison Bill."

"Maybe," Mary retorted, "but what possible motive did he have?"

"I don't know," Harriet grudgingly conceded. "God, it's frustrating!"

"And yet you were a witness that night," Shaefer noted. "You were seated near Mr. Holbrook. Did you not see anything suspicious? Think carefully—was there any particular time that would have been a good chance to poison him?"

Harriet cradled her head in her hands at that.

"I don't know," she answered, her voice full of regret and aggravation. "I really don't know! That night, the food and drinks just kept on coming and coming. Dish after dish just kept passing around. Someone was always there to fill your cup or pass you a new cup. I ate and drank things without any notion who was serving me."

"Do you at least remember who was there that night?" Mary gently asked.

Harriet gave a bitter laugh.

"Everyone was there that night! Well, literally everyone in town I've met," she amended. "There may be some shut-ins somewhere who were absent. But from I what could see, everyone in Munier who could stand was at the Feast that night. And quite a few people from outside town even. Like the gypsies!"

"Gypsies?" Mary wondered. "Real ones?"

"I think so," Harriet answered. "One of them claimed to be a fortune teller and even set up a booth. I actually paid her to have my cards read—just for fun, mind you!" She gave an uncomfortable laugh. "I don't really go in for that sort of thing, you know."

"Let me guess—she told you you'd soon meet a tall dark stranger?" Mary jested.

"Close. She foresaw trials and tribulations with an important journey in my future." Harriet stopped speaking and got a peculiar look on her face.

"What?" Mary wondered.

"She told me I was soon going to be reunited with an important figure from my past," Harriet murmured, looking anywhere other than at Mary. "And she told me I'd have to make an important decision."

Mary felt the heat rise to her cheeks and suddenly regretted the lack of any form of alcohol at the table. Shaefer looked back and forth between the two beautiful and now very uncomfortable-looking women dining with him and made a very artificial-sounding cough.

"Getting away from the question of whether sooth-saying is ever real," he said smoothly, "let's return to the actual dinner. You really didn't notice anything of use?" His voice held no audible reproach, but Harriet bridled a bit anyway.

"No!" she objected. "I told you. Now I'd been drinking a bit myself, but even if I hadn't been, the way they set it up that night, it was impossible to keep track of where anything was going. Good lord." Harriet's face grew fearful. "What if Bill wasn't even the intended victim at all? What if someone tried to give a dish to someone that Bill got by mistake? Or the killer just poisoned something at the table and left it to chance whoever got it!"

"Ah." Shaefer nodded sagely. "I am afraid that is also entirely possible. Mass poisoners sometimes do strike randomly. Though if that is the case, then in all likelihood the poisoner in question would not stop with only one victim. Having succeeded once, they would ply their craft again and again until they were caught."

Harriet looked alarmed. "Good lord, are you saying some madman—"

"Or woman," Shaefer helpfully corrected her. "Many mass poisoners are female. Lucrezia Borgia in Italy, Sophie Ursinus in Germany, Catherine Monvoisin in France." He checked the names off on his fingers.

"Mary Anne Cotton in England," Mary recalled.

"Correct!" Shaefer nodded in approval. "In fact, poison is usually the weapon of choice for women." He stroked his chin thoughtfully. "Perhaps because it requires no physical strength or even necessarily direct confrontation at all. It's quite an interesting field of research for psychiatrists. But never mind that." He shook his head. "Such speculation is useless when we have no knowledge of the gender of the killer, much less their motive."

"But whether it's a madman, a madwoman, or the Mad Hatter, there's a chance someone out there right now might be planning to poison more people?" Harriet turned ashen. "And here we are out eating and drinking food made in a public restaurant?" She shoved her plate and glass away from her with a look of horror.

"We don't know that is the case," Mary pointed out. "It could still have been a targeted attack on Holbrook himself. We just don't know!" She crossed her arms in irritation. "We're confoundingly ignorant here."

"Not entirely ignorant." Shaefer played devil's advocate. "We have already learned quite a bit about the deceased and about this town and that is not nothing. I suggest we continue to glean as much information as we can on both. And while a random attack is not something we can dismiss, for the sake of our current investigation I think it would be easier to focus on possible motives to kill Mr. Holbrook. After all, if his poisoning was just the beginning of a killing spree, more bodies will turn up soon anyway and we can deal with it then."

"Well said," Mary agreed. "But in the meantime, perhaps we should not be eating anything we don't prepare ourselves."

CHAPTER TEN

It was much to the astonishment of old Gaston that his current lodgers came back that afternoon armed with bags of tinned foods and packaged snacks they'd bought at the local store. He was even more surprised by their request that all these provisions be stored in a locked cupboard in the pantry. And he was outright speechless at their declaration they would not drink wine or anything else in the future that they hadn't poured and/or opened the bottle of themselves. The old man took it as the worst sort of insult. What kind of innkeeper would he be after all if he allowed any guest on his property to imbibe poison? His sense of honor—and hospitality—

was far too great for such a thing. Nevertheless, he accepted their decision, though his demeanor toward them grew cooler.

"We're in France, and we can't even enjoy the food," Harriet mourned.

"It's not a holiday, it's an investigation," Mary avowed firmly. "Once we've got the killer, we can go anywhere we like to celebrate. Or rather," she amended her statement seeing the slight twitch in Harriet's eye at the use of "we," "*you* can celebrate anywhere you like."

They heard the telltale sound of a car engine outside and both instinctively raced to the door to look.

"My god, it's the Peugeot!" Mary gasped.

"Did Jorisse decide to stay on after all?" a perplexed Harriet asked, but as the vehicle parked, they saw its only occupant was Raoul the driver. By that point, Shaefer had joined them outside looking equally perplexed. Raoul exited the car, and Harriet began quickly interrogating him in French. She received the following explanation.

Soon after leaving the outskirts of Munier behind in the distance, Jorisse had begun to have second thoughts. Not about leaving the town—the advocate had been adamant his personal presence was no longer needed. But he had worried about leaving Harriet and her friends without transport. So instead of having Raoul drive him all the way to Paris, he had instructed the driver to take him to the nearest train station where he could book a first-class ticket for the rest of the trip, then bid Raoul return to Munier where he and the Peugeot could be at their disposal.

"Well, how generous and thoughtful of him!" Mary exclaimed, and Harriet translated for Raoul who then answered.

"He says Jorisse said to tell him to tell us that he's going to charge us both for his train ticket to Paris and Raoul's wages for his time here," Harriet announced. "Also, there will be an additional surcharge for the use of the car."

"Fair enough," Mary noted, and Raoul spoke again.

"He also says his employer indicated he doesn't want Raoul gone with the car for too long either."

"All the more important then, that we move quickly," Shaefer opined. "If Raoul is not too tired, perhaps he can offer us a lift to the chateau?"

This got to the heart of why it was such a good thing to have Raoul return with the car. Alternate means of transportation back and forth from the chateau and surrounding estate probably could have been arranged if absolutely necessary. But it undoubtedly would have been difficult and time-consuming. They might well have ended up stuck traveling on the back of a hay cart drawn by a single flatulent horse, with a moldy old blanket the sole protection from the elements. Having a nice clean, warm car on hand was far more convenient and comfortable. Better still, a car driven by a driver who could be counted on to remain sober while on duty.

As said driver pleaded a need for nourishment, they waited for him to grab a sandwich and coffee from Gaston before setting off again. Mary had had Harriet translate to Raoul the suggestion that he might want to join them in their policy of eating only food straight from packaging, but the latter had adamantly refused. It is very difficult to put any true Frenchman off his diet, and Raoul was inclined to think his passengers were being far too paranoid. Bad enough he wasn't on the road back to Paris but instead playing chauffeur/babysitter to foreigners of suspect character. He'd be damned if let them starve him as well! Besides, he would never dream of insulting Gaston's hospitality like that.

When they finally did set out, the ride over was a solemn one. Mary and Shaefer were silent as they considered what approach to take with the Dellaires and Harriet was quite absorbed in her own thoughts as well.

"Actually," Shaefer spoke up, "let's not go to the chateau first. Harriet, can you instruct Raoul that we need to make a stop at the cottage of Fronsac first? I assume you know where his cottage is?"

"Of course!" Harriet answered, looking bewildered. "But why do you want to speak with him first? Do you think he killed Bill?"

"Just tell Raoul where to go," Shaefer replied obliquely.

Harriet did so while giving Mary a pointedly irritated look. The latter shrugged back at her as if to say, "What can I do? He's always like this!" In actuality, Mary already had a fair idea why Shaefer wanted to speak with Fronsac first. It had been obvious the night before that there was something the painter wasn't telling them, and Shaefer no doubt hoped to worm it out of him by questioning him without Madame Dellaire present.

Harriet directed Raoul to a side path from the main road that seemed little more than loose dirt that soon coated the sides of the Peugeot. It was clear at the end of this trip Raoul was going to have to give the car a good wash and shine despite having done so the day before leaving Paris. Yet another thing for the chauffeur to resent.

About a mile in, they found themselves at a stone

structure that looked a lot like the cluster of bories Mary and Shaefer had seen earlier, only slightly larger in scale with a second floor. The land surrounding it was quite a pretty area even by the standards of Provence. Off the road near the tree line, they could see wild blackberry bushes. Presumably the ones whose berries Fronsac had picked for the chateau which could be made out vaguely in the distance.

The cottage was settled just between the road and the forest. Its stone was very old and weathered with growths of lichen within the mortar. It was as if the whole property seemed melded with the roots of the trees surrounding it. Any stranger coming across it in the woods would be forgiven for thinking the property completely uninhabited. It was a cold day and the wind threatened to blow again at any time, yet there was no woodsmoke coming from the chimney. Nor were there any sounds, but rather the cottage was as still as a churchyard at night. Except for a discarded can of kerosene half buried in the high grass, it seemed utterly unchanged since the time of the doomed Templars. Well, that and the sound of gunfire off in the distance; presumably someone out hunting wild boar, but given Mary and Shaefer's profession, they couldn't help but automatically consider darker explanations.

"You're sure this it?" Mary's tone was skeptical as she tried to focus on what was in front of her rather than the ominous rifle noises.

"Yes," Harriet replied. "I've visited a couple of times. Fronsac's just not much for keeping a garden." She gestured toward the overgrown landscape apparently untouched by hoe or plow for generations.

Harriet, Shaefer, and Mary walked to the door while Raoul stayed behind to enjoy a smoke.

"Fronsac?" Harriet called out. "We've just come by to say hello!" There was no answer.

"I'll try the door anyway," Mary suggested, and she made a loud rap on the cracked wood—only for it swing inward an inch. "It's unlocked!"

"He must have just forgotten to lock it," Harriet murmured uneasily as if trying to convince herself. "We should probably try back later—hey!"

Mary had chosen not to wait but rather make her way into the cottage. The first thing she laid eyes on in the room was the figure of Fronsac sprawled on the floor, with a corkscrew sticking out of his chest.

CHAPTER ELEVEN

There was no phone at the cottage, so Harriet and Raoul drove off to the chateau to ring the police. Both were more than happy to leave yet another cursed place of bloodshed behind them in the rearview mirror. Raoul was reflecting bitterly that he was not getting paid nearly enough for this particular assignment and was going to have to demand a bonus from Jorisse once he returned to Paris. Harriet's thoughts were darker still. To say it had been a bad year for Harriet would have been a royal understatement. She had endured loss, heartbreak, betrayal, and numerous brushes with acts of violence even before her recent arrest. She was starting to wonder if she might be jinxed; that somehow, she brought darkness and death into the orbit anywhere she went. True, she hadn't been particularly familiar with the deceased painter, but still, that another person she knew should meet such a horrific end! She shivered, and it wasn't just the November cold.

Meanwhile, Mary and Shaefer stayed behind; officially to secure the scene and unofficially so they could nose and poke about to their hearts' content. Shaefer was, of course, an old hand at examining murdered bodies. Mary, while not quite so familiar—yet—was finding herself increasingly inured to the duty as well. Something she felt a mixture of guilt and relief about. At least Fronsac did not appear to have suffered; rather his face was frozen in a look of complete surprise. His death had been so immediate he hadn't had time to realize what was happening. In that respect, he'd been far luckier than Bill Holbrook. She put a hand on his neck and found the body ice cold.

"He's been dead for some time," she said. "Probably since last night. Damn, if only we'd pressed him harder when we saw him at the restaurant!"

"Hindsight is always so clear, is it not?" Shaefer sighed. "But we are in the business of detection not prophecy. By the way, do you have gloves on hand?"

She and Shaefer both quickly put on gloves.

"Good." Shaefer nodded. "Now that we won't leave any fingerprints, let's see how much we can learn before Inspector Bruno gets here."

"Not a doctor, and we'd need an autopsy, but cause of death seems pretty obvious." Mary gestured to the corkscrew. "A single strong blow to the chest from the looks of it. And one that took him completely by surprise. There's no sign of any defensive wounds on him."

She turned her attention from the corpse to examine the rest of the room, which was an untidy jumble of paint pots, canvases, wooden frames, and brushes. There was a persistent smell of turpentine in the room and what looked to be paint thinner in an old coffee jar. Almost every inch of the earthen floor was carpeted by a seemingly endless supply of yellowed newspapers and magazines. Half-melted candles occupied old wine jugs. Old sardine tins were used for makeshift ashtrays. There was a coat rack with a mannequin head on top that housed a couple of shabby cloaks, a spare smock, and a hat on the mannequin's head. A mortar and pestle lay on the floor—presumably what Fronsac had used to mix his homemade pigments. Jars of colored powders adorned a stray shelf. Framed paintings were piled up in one corner, and a few were displayed on the walls. Even to

Mary's untrained eye, the landscapes in question showed a good use of color and proportion.

"No other signs of a struggle either," Shaefer said, looking around. "Though in the general mess, it would be hard to tell." His eyes wandered to a small table toward the back of the room. "Look!" On the table under a faded blue velvet cloth lay two rather dingy-looking glasses and a single wine bottle unlabeled and unopened.

"He got the corkscrew out to open the bottle and pour out the wine," Mary said as realization dawned.

"Not only did he know his killer, but he was familiar enough with him to offer him a drink," Shaefer pronounced. "Admittedly here in France, people offer up drinks to guests all the time but still!"

"He couldn't have been afraid of his killer, then." Mary continued the chain of thought. "Which likely means Fronsac didn't suspect his guest of killing of Bill Holbrook or he'd have been more on guard. But he must have known something, or why else would he have been killed?"

"It certainly beggars belief that his death so soon after Holbrook's was a coincidence," Shaefer agreed. "Though, interestingly this was done with an entirely different choice of weapon. Assuming that"—he gestured toward the chest wound—"really is the famous Laguiole corkscrew he was so fond of, it means the killer improvised with what was close to hand."

"So, the murder may not have been premeditated?" Mary mused. "But Fronsac said or did something to set his assailant off."

"That would be my first supposition. Of course, there is another possibility. The perpetrator came with murder on their mind to begin with—maybe even had the poison in their pocket. And then on the spur of the moment decided to use the corkscrew instead." He looked thoughtful. "After all, poison requires stealth and distraction. You have to find a time when the victim isn't looking to put the poison in their glass."

"Which is a lot more difficult when it's just the two of you in a cozy meeting rather than a large, noisy festival," Mary surmised. "So, the corkscrew may have just seemed easier."

"Precisely!" Shaefer looked on her with proud approval. "Nevertheless, if I were Inspector Bruno, I'd have everything in here tested for poison. Including that bottle." He gestured to the still unopened wine bottle on the table.

"Look here!" Mary exclaimed, pulling out a sketchbook from the midst of the clutter. The pages of the book contained numerous drawings of female nudes. A woman standing au naturel against the wall looking out of the window. A woman sprawled out on a mattress. The woman wearing a mask for a fancy ball and nothing else. It soon became apparent the sketches were all of the exact same female, but the face was always turned away from the artist. The faceless model, whoever she was, had a very fine figure.

"Well, they're certainly...evocative," Mary opined with a flush in her cheeks.

Shaefer raised an eyebrow as well. "He undoubtedly had talent." He glanced at the body still before them. "And an appreciation for beauty!" He looked around at the other paintings with fresh eyes.

"Who was she?" Mary wondered, still transfixed by the nude drawings.

"A model he met in Paris or some other town perhaps?" Shaefer guessed. "Put the sketchbook down, though—Bruno will want everything to seem untouched!"

Mary obeyed his firm instruction.

By unspoken consensus, they started rummaging through the rest fof the cottage. They found nothing of any particular interest in the tiny kitchen; most of the pots and pans were dusty. It appeared that Fronsac had lived almost entirely on bread, cheese, and pickles bought in town. Upstairs revealed a bedroom that consisted of nothing more than a mattress on the floor, well-worn bedding, and a couple of books in French. *La Demoiselle aux yeux verts* by Maurice LeBlanc and *Les faux-monnayeurs* by Andre Gide. Mary carefully flipped through both but found no hidden letters or notes of any kind except a stray charcoal sketch of the cottage itself; evidently done at nighttime because of the pale moon hidden behind dark shadows. There was a little coal brazier in the corner which presumably came in handy on cold nights.

Overall, the bedroom had an austere feeling to it in sharp contrast to the jumbled nature of the downstairs living space. One got the sense that Fronsac had used the space for little more than actual sleeping. A quick examination of the closet revealed the late artist had mostly piled his clothes in a couple of baskets lying on top of each other rather than bother hanging them up. Mary rifled through the baskets but found nothing except for a few spare sous in a pair of trousers and a passport. The passport revealed no new information except a Parisian address and evidence of a trip to Spain a few years back before the civil war. Mary copied it all down anyway in her notebook. She was starting to feel frustrated at the lack of solid clues. Might Fronsac have carried something significant on his person? Possibly, but Mary wasn't sure how she felt about rifling through a dead man's pockets, much less whether Shaefer would approve of such a course of action. The latter meanwhile had been carefully inspecting the folds of the bedcovers.

"What's that?" Shaefer pointed at a spot of something bright buried in the blankets just before Mary could ask him his thoughts on robbing—or rather searching—the dead. He took out a pair of tweezers and carefully untangled a single tissue blotted with lipstick. So, Fronsac had in fact used the space for at least one other thing besides sleeping.

"Well, well, could this have belonged to Fronsac's mystery model?" he mused.

Mary started.

"My god, the lipstick—the shade—I recognize it!" she blurted out. "It's the same shade Angelique Farigoule wears!"

"The mayor's wife! Are you sure?"

"About it being the same lipstick color, yes!" Mary retorted. "But there are plenty of other women who wear it as well. Especially in the movies. But I haven't seen any others around Munier. It's more a city thing, that particular shade. Like something worn by women in Paris or Marseilles rather than out here in the sticks!"

"And Angelique Farigoule is from Marseilles," Shaefer said, following along.

"And according to Duvall, Fronsac once asked Angelique to sit for him as a model, but her husband said no," Mary recalled. "Perhaps she decided to take her own initiative on the matter."

"All highly suggestive. But not conclusive." At Mary's face, Shaefer reiterated, "Not conclusive for purposes of a courtroom anyway. Any decent lawyer would claim Fronsac was being visited by another woman from one of the places he sold his artwork. Or, for that matter, Fronsac might have enjoyed making up his own face from time to time. What? I saw it all the time in Berlin!"

"And I've seen it in London too," Mary noted. "But I don't think that was the case here."

"No. But sadly, we cannot actually prove otherwise. And it is the mayor's wife we'd be accusing," he cautioned as he carefully put the tissue with the tweezers back upon the blankets.

"What, you're just leaving it?" Mary protested. "It's evidence!"

"Exactly," Shaefer answered. "And we have no right to remove evidence from an active crime scene before Inspector Bruno gets here. We're already pushing it with this search."

"Do you think Inspector Bruno will draw the same conclusions we have? And even if he did, would he even be willing to consider the Farigoules suspects at all?" Mary wondered.

"Quite possibly not. But remember we have no jurisdiction here."

"We never have jurisdiction!" Mary pointed out.

"True," Shaefer conceded, "but at least in England we sometimes have local authorities or contacts who ask for assistance."

"And you have friends at Scotland Yard, if I recall correctly."

"Correct. But I don't have any such connections here in France and neither do you," he retorted. "Now, if Inspector Bruno asks for our assistance that would be one thing."

"He's not going to ask for our help," Mary broke in. "Not a puffed-up bullying little fool like him."

"Exactly! Not only can we not expect any cooperation on this case, but we must also tread carefully for fear of being arrested ourselves for interference and obstruction," Shaefer warned her. Somewhere in the distance, they heard a motor engine.

"Speak of the devil," Mary muttered, and she and Shaefer quickly went downstairs and stood by the door as if they'd stayed there the whole time. A police van deposited a red-faced Bruno and very dejected-looking Etienne on the side of the cottage.

"Where is he?" Bruno demanded of Shaefer, not addressing Mary at all. The former simply pointed inside to where the corpse lay.

"Très bien," Bruno pronounced. "You two can now leave this to Etienne and myself." As he spoke, he unconsciously puffed out his chest a bit.

"Will Dr. Aubert be conducting the post-mortem?" Shaefer asked casually.

"That's not your concern," Bruno snapped as Etienne responded, "Oui, she has already been called."

"Merci." Mary gave Etienne a warm smile of encouragement to counteract Bruno's scowl. "We'd better go!" And she and Shaefer hurriedly took their leave.

CHAPTER TWELVE

Once more, Shaefer and Mary were without a car. Fortunately, it was not a very long walk from Fronsac's cottage to the chateau, and it gave them time to talk.

"You seemed anxious that Dr. Aubert be the one to conduct the autopsy," Mary noted.

"Correct. Clear cause of death or not, I still want to learn anything the medical examiner can tell us. After all," he noted wryly, "we've just seen how crucial that was in the case of Mr. Holbrook."

"Well, yes, I figured that," Mary answered impatiently. "I just wasn't sure why it mattered to you it be Dr. Aubert. She didn't exactly give us the warmest reception, did she?"

"No, but she didn't refuse us either, did she?" Shaefer retorted. "Besides, I suspect Dr. Aubert is not especially warm to most people, so there is no reason we should take it personally."

Mary couldn't help but laugh a bit at that. One thing anyone working in the medical field soon realized was that surgeons as a group were remarkably devoid of feeling. Why should that not be true for women doctors as much as the men?

The temperature was chilly, and Mary was glad she'd worn a sweater. Within the last ten minutes of their walk, they began to sense an ominous change in the air about them. Sure enough, the mistral had returned in full malevolence. Shaefer swore a litany of German curses as he clutched his hat, and Mary tried her best to keep her head down out of the full force of the wind. Thus it was they arrived at the main entrance of the chateau with mussed hair and chattering teeth.

Shaefer pressed down on the doorbell as hard as he could.

It was Armand who let them in with a vaguely disapproving look. Not so much for the disheveled state of their appearance but for their poor taste in coming to the chateau straight from a grisly crime scene.

"The driver Raoul is in the kitchen," he informed them. "Mademoiselle West is in the drawing room recuperating."

"And what about Madame Dellaire?" Mary asked him.

"Alas, Madame is quite unavailable. She has taken the death of Fronsac very hard, particularly after the news Monsieur Holbrook was poisoned. She's locked herself in her chambers and will see no one." Armand spoke with just a hint of reproach that suggested he personally held Mary and Shaefer responsible for the unhealthy shocks to his mistress's constitution.

"I understand if she won't see us," Shaefer commented. "But Inspector Bruno will almost certainly want to question her as well."

"We shall see," Armand sniffed, as if to say the inspector would see Madame only when she was ready and no sooner. "Do you want me to take you to Miss West?"

Harriet sat in the same blue-and-white parlor where they originally had met Madame Dellaire. Before her lay a teacup, a tea kettle, and a decanter of brandy which she'd made hearty use of to fortify her tea.

"Thank god!" she exclaimed at the sight of Mary. "It's been bad here, Mary. Really bad." She tugged her hair with anxiety, and Mary instinctively sat down beside her and put a consoling hand upon her shoulder.

"Armand told us Madame was so upset she locked herself in her room."

"She was crying!" Harriet blurted out. "I've never seen her cry before. But when she heard what happened to Fronsac...it's like it all swelled up in her at once. She just fell to pieces and started talking about how the curse had come back again."

"Always the Templar curse," Shaefer muttered. "It looms so large in the minds of everyone here."

"She ran upstairs, and I had to ask Armand to take me to the phone," Harriet continued. "Meanwhile, that rat Raoul jumped ship and ran off to the kitchen. Said he needed coffee. Just abandoned me all alone." Harriet gnashed her teeth as Mary refrained from pointing out Raoul's actions hardly constituted "abandonment." Harriet had, after all, suffered quite a shock on top of a particularly bad week. One could hardly expect her to be fully reasonable. Harriet poured some of the brandy into the teacup and gulped it down.

"Well, that's enough of that then." Mary picked up the decanter and moved it across the room out of Harriet's reach.

"God," Harriet moaned. "I forgot how much of a bloody mother hen you can be! Next, you'll be serving me hot milk and reminding me to eat my vegetables."

"Have you been eating them?" Mary asked innocently, and Harriet was irked until she saw the merriment in her eyes.

"All right, for a moment you had me!" She laughed.

"Ahem." Shaefer gave one of the loudest throat clearings of his life, and both women started rather guiltily. "Has Maxim Dellaire been informed of Fronsac's death?"

"I believe one of the servants was sent to hunt him down on the estate and tell him," Harriet answered.

"I want to speak with him," Shaefer declared.

"You don't think Maxim killed Bill and Fronsac, do you?" Harriet looked shocked and excited at the same time.

"At present I think nothing," Shaefer replied. "But Maxim may be one of the few people who can offer any information about the matter. Apart from you, of course."

"Me!" Harriet's mouth dropped.

"You knew him, did you not? Just as you knew Bill Holbrook."

"Not quite like I knew Bill," Harriet corrected him. "Fronsac and I never went to bed together."

"But still you were acquainted with both men and spoke to them personally," Shaefer reminded her. "It is perhaps a good thing you were still in prison last night, as that at least clears you of his murder."

"You're joking!" Harriet snapped.

"Sadly no." Shaefer shook his head. "Technically you're not even entirely in the clear yet in the death of Bill Holbrook. They could always say you'd been the one to administer the poison to him in the first place, before pushing him to finish the job. Not that they will," he quickly amended. "Not now at any rate. After all, you have the best possible alibi for the death of Fronsac, and even Inspector Bruno would have trouble suggesting those crimes were unconnected."

"Good lord," Harriet realized. "I'm going to have to talk to Bruno again, aren't I? He'll want to question me about Fronsac."

"Probably," Mary asserted. "But at least you won't be in handcuffs this time."

"What Bruno will demand of you will be any possible connection between the deaths of Holbrook and Fronsac," Shaefer pronounced. "Who could possibly have wanted to kill both men?" He affixed Harriet with a long gaze.

"I don't know!" she cried out in earnest. "I truly

don't know. I told you before, I really had no notion why anyone would want to kill Bill and even less idea for why they'd harm Fronsac. Honestly, the man was a hermit except for his art."

"A hermit who was bedding the mayor's wife," Mary remarked.

"What?" Harriet looked agog. "Are you sure?"

"Not absolutely, but it seems pretty likely." And Mary gave a quick recount of their findings at Fronsac's cottage.

"So that's a good motive for Mayor Farigoule to kill Fronsac," Mary concluded.

"But why kill Bill then?"

"Maybe Bill was the one he first suspected," Mary pondered. "He knew his wife had a lover, but he wasn't sure who. Other people saw Holbrook talking to Madame Farigoule and drew the wrong conclusions. Maybe the mayor did the same."

"Maybe that was even deliberate on Angelique's part." Harriet's eyes narrowed in concentration. "Maybe she flirted publicly with Bill to draw attention away from what she was really up to. Classic French diversionary tactic, you know," she observed with a twinge of admiration.

"Quite possibly," Mary said. "But after Holbrook's

death, maybe the mayor learned the truth and the second time around he targeted the right man for death. Or paid someone to do it for him. And we can't rule Angelique out as a suspect either. Bill might have found out about the affair, so she decided to get rid of him."

"And then killed Fronsac to silence him forever too?" Harriet looked skeptical.

"Possibly. Or Fronsac might have just been a lovers' quarrel. After all, the killer did use a weapon of opportunity on that occasion," Mary mused.

"And then there's the old rumor about Madame Dellaire murdering her husband. Maybe Bill suspected something. Or Fronsac did," Harriet thought aloud. "Or they worked it out together, which is why they both had to die."

"Fascinating as all this is," Shaefer interrupted, "I must remind you that we have no evidence linking either the Farigoules or the Dellaire family to the killings. And it could be...risky to make any public accusations against them," he cautioned.

"You're right," Harriet conceded. "Accusing the mayor and his wife of murder in a town like this could get you lynched. The only thing worse would be to call the local priest a suspect."

"Unless he has an alibi," Shaefer pointed out

wryly, "we can't be sure he isn't." Mary and Harriet both assumed he was joking, but neither could detect any hint of mirth on his visage. "After all," he continued with a perfectly straight face. "Perhaps the priest disapproved of their morals and decided to take old-fashioned retribution."

"Now I know you're joking," Mary reproached him.

"In this case, yes, but not always." Shaefer looked thoughtful. "How many people have committed murder solely out of moral disapproval of the victim?"

"Sixth commandment clearly states, 'Thou Shall Not Kill,'" Mary reminded him. "Even I know that."

"And I am sure that was a great consolation to victims of the Spanish Inquisition," Shaefer retorted smartly.

"I think we've moved forward a bit since then," Mary argued.

"According to whom?" Shaefer countered.

"And now who's getting off the current subject with speculations we can't prove?" Harriet interjected. She found herself inexplicably irritated by Mary and Shaefer's banter. She, better than almost anyone else, knew there would never be anything romantic between the two, but their natural rapport otherwise could make you feel a bit like a third wheel. It wasn't that Harriet particularly wanted to be an investigator herself, but no one likes feeling left out. In fact, she now privately admitted to herself it was one of the reasons she hadn't liked Mary agreeing to be Shaefer's assistant. How must either of Dr. Watson's two wives have felt about having to share their spouse with Sherlock Holmes? It wasn't something Sir Arthur Conan Doyle ever thought to address and in retrospect Harriet now considered that a large omission on his part.

This chain of thought was broken up by the arrival of yet another familiar face. Maxim Dellaire tromped into the parlor in mud-splattered boots, much to Armand's dismay, his face chapped by wind and his blood-shot eyes those of a madman.

"Is it true?" he shouted. "Is Fronsac truly dead?"

"Yes." Mary spoke up despite his evidently stormy mood. "Yes, he is. I saw his body myself." As she spoke, it was as if Maxim were a balloon someone had punctured with a pin. All the body seemed to go out of him, and he shrank into a shadow of himself. He did not so much sit himself in one of the chairs as collapse into it. Mary grabbed the brandy decanter she had earlier seized from Harriet and poured Maxim a large glass, which he accepted with a barely audible "Merci," then downed in a single gulp.

Harriet felt a moment's resentment that Mary was willing to treat other people's distress with alcohol but not hers. Then she felt ashamed for having such a selfish thought in the face of Maxim Dellaire's obvious—and unexpected—level of pain. She was no newcomer to grief herself. Even so, she didn't know how to give Maxim comfort beyond offering liquor. So, she instinctively left it to Mary, as did Shaefer.

Mary took her gaze off Maxim for but a moment to look at them both. "Leave!" She mouthed her command silently to them both, and Shaefer was the first to stand up and quietly make his exit. Harriet hesitated a moment, looking unsure, but then followed Shaefer. Mary put a comforting hand on Maxim's shoulder and left it there, simply standing quietly in wait.

Her patience was rewarded after a few minutes when Maxim was the first to break the silence.

"Did he suffer?" he asked. His voice was choked, as if he were barely holding in tears.

"No," Mary told him firmly. "Death was immediate. He wouldn't have had time for pain or fear."

"Grace à Dieu," he muttered. "I do not think I could have borne if he had... I could not." Then came the tears. Mary said nothing but handed him her handkerchief with one hand while she pressed his shoulder even harder with the other.

"I'm sorry," he told her eventually as he dried his eyes. "Foolish weakness on my part!"

"No, it wasn't. It is neither foolish nor weak to grieve. I don't understand why men always think otherwise."

Maxim's lips twisted into a half-smile.

"I thought you English believed in stoicism. The 'stiff upper lip,'" he quoted ironically.

"For some things I do." Mary gazed at him. "There's no use in getting worked up over trifles. But this isn't a trifle now, is it? After all, you loved him." It was a simple statement of fact. But in it lay worlds.

"Yes," Maxim whispered. "Yes, I did." He looked almost shocked to even say the words, as if he thought the roof and walls of the chateau would suddenly cave in on him. But they did not. And his listener was not disgusted or even shocked by his statement. She just looked at him with the same compassionate eyes he'd seen in paintings of the Virgin Mary.

"Did Fronsac know?" she asked quietly.

"No," Maxim declared. "I never said anything. He was...he was not like me. I could tell."

"I see," Mary answered. "So instead, you loved

from afar." She knew something of that; it had been the case for her and a number of her fellow schoolgirls in her youth. She'd been fortunate enough when she went to London to find others like herself in whose arms she'd been able to take comfort. But for someone like Maxim, wedded to the land, it would have been much harder to find company.

"Not so very far," Maxim told her. "We were friends. He was happy to be my friend at least." His lip trembled a bit. "I didn't dare let him find out I wanted anything else. It would have ruined everything."

"Fronsac liked women," Mary noted.

"Oui," Maxim replied. "Ironic, is it not?" He didn't wait for an answer. "I've heard people say it is artistes and sophisticates in cities who are deviants as opposed to us honest country folk. But so far as I know Fronsac's appetites were normal for men of his age while I..." He gazed off into the distance for a moment, and again Mary marveled at how profound Maxim's loneliness must be as he finally found his voice once more. "When he went to Avignon and Marseilles, it was not just to sell his paintings but for feminine company. They have some excellent brothels in both towns," Maxim commented as if he were reporting on cheese sales. "Fronsac always said he preferred not to get involved with any of the local mesdames. Said it would be too much trouble." A note of bitter jealousy entered his voice. "That is what he said!"

"But you think he did anyway," Mary thought aloud, and Maxim nodded.

"One time, I saw a woman leave his cottage. But I saw her only from a distance, and she was cloaked so I could not see who. Une femme mysterieuse just like the cinema, eh?" He looked angry at the recollection. "In the movies, it is always une femme mysterieuse who kills the man. Do you think that is what happened to Fronsac?" he demanded of Mary who chose her next words carefully.

"What more can you tell me about the lady in the cloak?" she asked.

"Rien," Maxim responded. "Nothing!" His mood shifted once again from anger back to sorrow. "After I see her, I ask him who it was, and he got angry. Told me it was none of my business even if it was my land! We did not speak again for several days. When we did start speaking once more, we never speak of the woman again like she did not exist." Clearly Maxim had no notion that Angelique Farigoule had been Fronsac's mystery mistress. At this point, Mary decided it was better not to tell him.

"What I tell you..." Maxim spoke hesitantly.

"I won't breathe a word to anyone else," Mary told him unprompted. "I promise."

"And you do not despise me for what I tell you?" Maxim marveled.

"Sometimes, we love people who don't love us back. We just can't help ourselves."

She must have given away more than she intended, for Maxim asked, "Do you love Mademoiselle West?"

"Yes," Mary answered right away.

"Does she love you?"

"I don't know." Mary brooded. "And even if she did, love might not be enough. It's very complicated, isn't it? Love. Especially for people like us," she observed sadly, and Maxim nodded.

"My aunt keeps asking me when I will marry and give the chateau an heir," he noted absently.

"She doesn't know?" Mary thought of Madame Dellaire's ill-conceived campaign to set Harriet up with Maxim.

"I think she does know," Maxim said with a frown. "I have said nothing. Done nothing. But I've seen her watch me sometimes when I am talking to the laborers, you understand? She frowns, and she asks me if I want to speak to the priest. So yes, she knows but she pretends not to. She never says what she thinks I might want to talk to the priest about. She cannot even say it aloud!"

Mary flinched. She thought about her own mother who had never met Harriet and never once said anything to indicate she knew her daughter was a lesbian. But even so, deep down, Mary felt sure her mother knew.

"Even knowing," Maxim went on, "she still thinks I should do my duty and marry. After all, she did hers when she married my uncle. And no one called that a happy marriage." He shook his head. "But when she and her husband both took other lovers no one cared. It is France after all, even if it is the country. But for me—and for you—" He looked at Mary. "It must always be the shadows. Why?"

She had no answer to give, and after that they sat in silence.

CHAPTER THIRTEEN

After informing Armand that Mademoiselle Grey and Maxim Dellaire should on no account be disturbed, Harriet and Shaefer went to the kitchen. They intended to reconnoiter with Raoul, but a quick glance revealed him to be in serious conversation with a kitchen maid. It didn't look like either of them wanted to be disturbed so Harriet and Shaefer gallantly walked away without announcing themselves, leaving them both at a bit of a loss.

"How well do you know this chateau by now?" Shaefer asked.

"Well enough to find my way around," she answered. "Why?"

"Would you care to give me a tour? It isn't one of our crime scenes, but I am curious."

"All right." Harriet nodded in agreement, if a bit bewildered by Shaefer's sudden interest. "First stop, the family gallery."

She led him into a hallway lined with large, heavy framed portraits of various members of the Dellaire family going back to the seventeenth century. It may have simply been the aesthetic choices of the various artists, but on the whole, they did not appear a very cheerful lot. Some, such as Jean-Louis Dellaire and his wife Blanche Marie, had ample cause for sorrow. The former had fallen victim to the guillotine while the latter had been spared only because of her pregnancy. An awfully large number of the faces on the walls had in fact met untimely deaths, including Madame Dellaire's late husband. Shaefer studied this most recent portrait with considerable interest. There was a strong resemblance between him and his nephew, but the uncle had had cruel eyes and a haughty sneer, which Maxim lacked.

"Not a nice looking fellow, was he?" Harriet reflected. "I don't know what would have possessed Madame to marry him in the first place."

"Family pressure perhaps?" Shaefer mused. "Or perhaps it was about the chateau and estate. The man himself may have been an unfortunate tag-along."

"Probably," Harriet agreed. "That's certainly the way it is in England, isn't it?" She was struck with a sudden realization. "My god, I barely escaped that same fate myself!" She shuddered at the thought of her previous and disastrous engagement to a member of the British nobility. If Lord Edgar Pool were still alive... She did not want to think about what married life with him would have entailed.

"I am surprised the portrait still hangs here," Shaefer went on. "If he could not be buried on consecrated land and the room he died in is locked up, why still hang his picture?"

"Don't know." Harriet frowned in bewilderment. "Tradition, I suppose?"

"Or perhaps a sort of warning?" Shaefer speculated. "Future Dellaire children will be taken here to see the portrait of their wicked ancestor. Assuming, of course, there are any future Dellaire children." He gave Harriet a significant look.

"I had no idea," she told him flatly. "I mean, I knew he wasn't interested in me, but I didn't know that. I'd make a horrible detective," she declared.

"Perhaps you had other things occupying your mind," he suggested.

"Let's see the rest of the house." Harriet evaded the question, and Shaefer knew better than to press her. She showed him where she'd been sleeping; a beautiful guest suite done up in delicate shades of lavender and green. On the wall hung a watercolor painting of a little girl in a white dress and blue ribbon holding a toy pug. There was a genuine Oriental carpet and a giant white-and-gold armoire with a full-length mirror, but the crowning glory was a magnificent oaken carved four-poster canopy bed.

Shaefer whistled. "Bit of a comedown for you to stay at the inn after this, wasn't it?" he jested.

"I liked it well enough while I was here. But I'm afraid all my memories of the chateau and the town are now tainted."

Yet, Shaefer wanted to point out, Harriet had voluntarily chosen to stay on in Munier anyway. He had a strong suspicion why, but he didn't vocalize it.

"Really," Harriet continued. "You should see Madame Dellaire's suite. Marie Antoinette herself could have lain there!"

"Unfortunately, I suspect if I tried to interrupt Madame in her quarters right now," Shaefer noted wryly, "she'd probably insist on having me thrown out altogether." He sighed. "I do not miss the paperwork of being an official policeman, but it was nice having actual authority to question people." He shook his head. "Ah well, can you show me now to the late Mr. Holbrook's room?"

Holbrook's room was as spacious as Harriet's had been but decorated in a more masculine, subdued style. There was an antique wooden desk and chair in one corner. It all looked comfortable except for one detail. On the wall hung a painting of a stag wounded by an arrow to the side. Over the stag loomed a rough-looking huntsman with a knife, clearly about to finish the beast off. Given Bill Holbrook's reaction to seeing Maxim take down the sanglier on his one and only hunting trip, it seemed doubtful he'd have enjoyed this particular piece of artwork.

Shaefer conducted a thorough search of the room to no avail. Since Holbrook's death, the room had not only been thoroughly cleaned by the staff, but Holbrook's effects had also been gathered up and sent off to his surviving kin. Upon learning this, Shaefer let loose a litany of German curses.

"It should have been thoroughly secured as a crime scene." He ground his teeth. "Even with a self-confessed killer in custody, his effects should have been preserved as evidence. Imbeciles! The lot of them."

"Well, if it's any consolation," Harriet suggested, "Bill didn't bring that much with him in any event. He was living out of a single suitcase he brought with him from Paris."

At that, Shaefer stopped in his tracks and stared at Harriet.

"What did you just say?" he whispered.

"Single suitcase?" Harriet guessed.

"No." Shaefer shook his head. "Paris! Bill Holbrook's primary address in France was in Paris."

"Yes. Yes, it was," a bewildered Harriet answered, "but how does that matter?"

"And Fronsac the painter was originally from Paris as well, wasn't he? In fact, that is how he first knew Bill Holbrook."

For Harriet, the light began to dawn. "And Fronsac was the one who got Bill invited to the chateau in the first place."

"How much do you know about Fronsac's life in Paris?" Shaefer asked.

Harriet had to think a bit.

"You know, now that you mention it, not a whole lot really," she replied slowly. "Oh, Bill liked talking up how much fun he'd had in Gay Paree...but Fronsac... I can't remember him ever speaking about it all. I remember once when we were all together at the café, Bill, Fronsac, Maxim, and me chatting over pastis and Bill started going on about how much partying he and Fronsac had done back in the city, Fronsac got really quiet and then left the table. After that, Bill never said a word about Paris again when Fronsac was around."

"Most intriguing," Shaefer told her. "And when Fronsac went to the cities to sell his paintings, Maxim said he went to dealers in Avignon and Marseilles. Not Paris. Rather odd, wasn't it? Given that Paris is where the most art dealers in France are."

"I never wondered," Harriet marveled at herself. "I just never even thought—how stupid of me!"

"If you weren't thinking then the rest of us weren't either," he assured her. "But what if we've been looking at this matter the wrong way around this entire time? What if the motive for both men's killings lies not here in Munier but in their shared past in the City of Lights? The way is now clear; to help learn the truth of what happened here in Munier, we must pay a visit to Paris."

*

Shaefer, Harriet, and Mary eventually reunited on the ground floor and, much to the delight of Armand and disappointment of Raoul, insisted on leaving at once.

Only when they started driving off in the Peugeot did Shaefer share with Mary that they needed to continue the investigation in Paris.

"But it's already getting dark, so we cannot set off tonight. We must return to the inn for now and then first thing in the morning we can set out," he reasoned.

"But what about the Farigoules?" Mary protested. "Shouldn't we still question them?"

"Probably." Shaefer had a sudden thought. "Tell me, is there any train in the area with overnight service to Paris?"

"There is," Harriet answered. "But the station is nearly an hour's drive from here and the last train leaves in little over an hour."

"Then tell Raoul to drive us there at once," Shaefer declared, and Harriet did so. "Here is the plan," he told them. "Mary—you will take the train to Paris and find out everything you can about Holbrook and Fronsac's lives there. I will have Raoul drive me back to the inn in Munier and continue our investigation here."

"Wait, you're sending me to Paris while you stay behind?" Mary was surprised and flattered. "You trust me that much?"

"I have full faith in your ability to scout out information in Paris on your own. Besides," he noted wryly, "in our last investigation, it was I who got to leave for the city and you got stuck behind in a small community with a murderer on a killing spree. It seems only fair we now reverse that order."

"Wait—when was this?" Harriet spoke up in alarm.

"Just before we came here," Shaefer answered absently. "Mary here stared down a particularly vicious axe killer all by herself!"

Mary couldn't help but preen with pride at that while Harriet simply stared slack-jawed at them both.

"Meanwhile," Shaefer went on, "Raoul must stay with me so I can at least have access to a car. After all," he mused, "it's probably a good idea for me to visit some of the dealers Fronsac met with in Avignon and Marseilles as well."

"And what about me?" Harriet piped up. "What am I going to do during all this?"

"Well, that would depend on you. You are welcome to stay behind in Munier and assist me. Or you can ride on to Paris with Miss Grey."

There was an awkward silence as they all waited for Harriet to make her choice. Finally, she came to a decision.

"I don't think I'm going to be much help as an investigator here or in Paris. But in Paris at least I'd have my choice of other things to do. There's not much for me in Munier, is there? Except apparently, the chance of having a showdown with a depraved killer," she added with considerable acidity.

"What about Inspector Bruno?" Mary blurted out. "Didn't he say he wanted you to stay in Munier?" She then felt like biting her tongue.

"True, but I refuse to let my movements be dictated by that fat Cossack anymore! I swear I can't see the end of him—or this damned village—fast enough. After all," she reasoned, "there's no reason he has to know I've left Munier. And even if he does find out"—and here a note of triumph crept into her voice—"that won't do him much good unless someone tells him where I actually am."

Mary wondered if Harriet wasn't being rash but knew from past experience it would be no use trying to talk her out of this opinion. Instead, she turned to Shaefer.

"But won't you need Harriet as your translator?" she asked.

"No, she can serve you in that department," Shaefer retorted. "I can just use Raoul. Isn't that right?" he addressed the chauffeur. "You do speak English, don't you?"

"Yes, I speak a little English," Raoul unflappably admitted as both Harriet and Mary's jaws dropped. "How did you guess?"

"From the very first day I suspected it. I could see you watching us talk through the rearview mirror-and sometimes react to what we said even though we spoke English. But it wasn't conclusively proven until just now when you made your fatal mistake."

"What mistake?" Raoul looked insulted.

"The direction you're driving. It's not the way back to the inn," Shaefer observed.

"I'll be damned," Harriet marveled. "He's right—we are heading west, not back into town."

"This, I believe," Shaefer continued, "is the way to the nearest train station where we needed to go. But you changed the car's direction before Miss West instructed you to do so in French!"

"All right, that was a mistake," Raoul admitted begrudgingly.

"Why have you spent the last few days pretending you didn't speak English?" Mary interrogated him.

"I never said I didn't speak English. You just assumed."

"Still a lie of omission." Mary's tone was tart.

"Lie of what?" Raoul asked.

"Oh, don't try to play innocent!" Mary retorted. "I bet you know perfectly well what a lie of omission is."

"It was Jorisse, wasn't it, who ordered you not to let on you spoke English?" Shaefer cut in.

Raoul mentally debated his options and finally decided to throw his employer to the foreign wolves.

"Yes," he confessed. "He thought it might be useful if I could listen to you speaking without you knowing I was listening. Pardon." He shrugged one shoulder while keeping his hands on the wheel.

"He asked you to spy on us?" Harriet was positively scandalized. "Why, that giant weasel... I ought to wring his neck. After I fire him!"

"Do nothing of the kind," Shaefer advised. "For one thing, he is still of use to us as is this car and Raoul. Moreover, one of the biggest problems lawyers have regardless of nationality is people not telling them the whole truth. Anyway, for Jorisse to get more candid information about Miss West, Miss Grey, or even myself was thus a most prudent effort on his part." He spoke with evident admiration.

"Quite the sly old fox then." Mary could not keep the amusement out of her voice.

"I still want a word with him," Harriet vowed. "That settles it." She turned to Mary. "We're going to

Paris!"

Nothing more was said for the rest of the drive. Raoul was too busy keeping his eyes on the road. Shaefer was too busy keeping his mind on the case. Mary was too busy trying to sort through her thoughts and feelings about traveling alone with Harriet. And Harriet was too busy stewing on the perfidy of the entire French legal establishment.

Finally, they turned a corner of the road and saw the lights of the train station. Mary and Harriet ran to the ticket office and ascertained there was still one first-class sleeper car available for Paris with two rollout beds. Mary let Harriet pay, and they boarded the train minutes before it was set to depart.

They first made a trip to the dining car to get a quick bite.

"Now that we're no longer officially on duty, I'd say we earned a drink as well," Harriet proclaimed, and before getting Mary's answer, told the server, "Whiskey sour, please. Quickly!"

"Just beer for me if you have any," Mary said.

"And for dinner how about a couple of croques monsieur?" Harriet added, and the server hurried off.

"Croaks what?" Mary looked alarmed. Was Harriet trying to make her eat frogs?

"They're just toasted ham and cheese sandwiches," Harriet assured her. At Mary's continued suspicious look, she added, "Oh for god's sakes, would I lie to you?"

Mary made no verbal response but folded her arms in an eloquent gesture.

"At least," Harriet noted cheerfully as their drinks arrived, "now that we're out of that wretched town, we don't have to worry about being poisoned anymore. Cheers!"

The croques monsieur arrived. Much to Mary's relief, they were indeed sandwiches. Very delicious sandwiches in fact.

"Why didn't you tell me about these before?" Mary wondered between mouthfuls.

"You needed to expand your horizons," Harriet argued in response.

"Says you!" Mary mouthed off before taking a hearty swig of the good strong beer she'd been served. She decided she liked it better than the pastis and ordered another one.

After being refreshed by the food and drink, they made their way to their sleeper compartment where the beds had already been turned down. It was only as they locked the door that Mary made a sudden realization.

"Good lord!" she exclaimed. "All my things are back at the inn. I haven't anything to wear but the clothes on my back."

"Neither do I," Harriet declared airily. "But no worries, there's no better place than Paris to replace a wardrobe. First thing when we arrive, I'll take you shopping."

"But—" Mary protested. Truth be told, Harriet's insistence on dressing her in the past had been one of the few things about their relationship Mary hadn't missed. Not that Harriet had ever picked out bad wardrobe selections for Mary: quite the opposite. But wearing such expensive garments had made Mary feel like a common pigeon trying on peacock feathers. Even the salesladies in the shops had sensed the incongruity and had looked dubious as Mary was ushered into the changing room. The women in French boutiques would almost surely be even worse.

"But nothing!" Harriet insisted. She had always been oblivious to Mary's discomfort with finery or, perhaps more accurately, dismissive of it. "You can certainly use a new outfit or two."

"Oh really?" Mary folded her arms and narrowed her eyes.

"I didn't mean it that way," Harriet told her. "I just

wanted to do something generous to repay you."

"But you don't have to."

"Oh yes, I do," Harriet told her softly, taking Mary's hand. "After all, you did cross the Channel on a moment's notice to come to my rescue."

"I'd always do that." Mary felt herself melting. "You know you can always rely on me when you're in trouble. Nothing will ever change that."

"I know." Harriet's eyes misted over. "You're like a Knight of the Round Table, aren't you? Always needing to rescue the helpless damsel in distress."

"Since when are you helpless?" Mary countered tartly. "And I'm afraid I don't have a suit of shining armor."

"I could always get you one," Harriet offered. "By way of a thank-you."

Mary gave her a good long look. "There are," she suggested, "better ways to thank me."

As it happened, while there were two beds available in the sleeping car that night, they only made use of one.

CHAPTER FOURTEEN

Shaefer's night was a far lonelier one. Upon dropping off Harriet and Mary at the train station, Raoul had driven him straight back to the inn. By that time, the mistral had begun to blow once more and Shaefer regretted not bringing something to protect his face from the cold sea wind. He and Raoul were immediately greeted by the always dour Gaston who had neither food nor drink to welcome them with. While this was exactly what Shaefer intended, a truly ravenous Raoul felt differently. He ran off to get refreshment at the nearby café before it closed, and Shaefer was left eating alone out of a tin can, in the drafty main room with a sullen innkeeper lurking in the shadows, prompting him to retire early. Fortunately, Shaefer had never come to France expecting a holiday, and he was an expert at brooding quietly in the darkness of his own room.

Among the many things he brooded about was his suspicion that Harriet West and Mary Grey were no doubt having a much better night on board the train. It was not that he was jealous exactly, but when one's own personal self has been lonely—and celibate—a long time, it doesn't help your mood to think of other people's couplings. When he got back to England, he was going to have to make more of an effort to meet someone. For now, though, he tried to focus on the case.

It was not something Shaefer would have liked to say aloud, but having a second murder in many ways improved the situation. At least purely from the puzzle-solving perspective. For the killing of Bill Holbrook, it seemed everyone in town had opportunity if not clear motive. With two killings, things became clearer. After all, who had the opportunity to kill both men? Already their list of suspects had narrowed; for instance, Harriet West was now in the clear. Not that Shaefer had considered her the most likely person to have poisoned Holbrook, but unlike Mary, he had been unable to dispense with the possibility entirely. Now he could, and honestly it was a relief to do so. Not just for Mary's sake but because Harriet was the one bankrolling this particular investigation. Hard to accuse someone of premeditated murder then present them with a bill for your services.

On that note, Shaefer fell asleep.

He awoke the next morning to a breakfast of dried biscuits from an unopened box. Gaston had not bothered to make coffee. Shaefer momentarily considered his options. Go without coffee or pay a visit to the café. After much internal agony he chose the former. It was thus in a very glum mood that he approached the mayor's house and rang the bell at the tradesmen's entrance with Raoul by his side to act as translator. They were greeted by a housekeeper who sharply informed them the Farigoules were indisposed. The mayor, it seemed, was in an emergency meeting with Inspector Bruno and other town notables about the sudden crime wave. And Angelique Farigoule, it was said, had retired inconsolable to her rooms with smelling salts.

"I think she will see me," Shaefer opined. "Tell her that I am interested in some drawings she posed for. That is all."

A baffled Raoul conveyed the message to the equally baffled housekeeper as they waited on the stoop.

Exactly two minutes later, the housekeeper returned to inform them that Madame was willing to speak to Shaefer. But only Shaefer and only in private. Raoul could take his choice of waiting in the kitchen or standing outside in the cold. He wisely chose the former and was rewarded with a mug of chocolate chaud by the cook.

Shaefer was taken directly to Angelique Farigoule's boudoir. The room was mostly decorated in very heavy respectable furnishings which looked as old as the building itself, and the thick velvet draperies had clearly lost some battles with moths. Angelique Farigoule, clad in a pink-and-green dressing gown, lay on a futon. She gave no hint of asking Shaefer to sit so he remained standing.

"Bonjour," she finally spoke though it was clear she begrudged his presence in her room.

"Bonjour," he replied politely. "Thank you for inviting me into your lovely home."

"Lovely home?" Her lips turned into a sneer, and red spots appeared in her cheeks. "Mon Dieu, I hate this place!" she spat out. "Everything is so old and ugly. Always I ask my husband—beg him—to let me redecorate. Always he say no. Say it is the way the house has always been and we must not change it. As if it were a museum. Or a shrine. Or worse still a mausoleum." Not just the words, but the tone of her voice was like pieces of shattered glass on a floor ready to cut any unwary soul at a moment's notice. Then, just as quickly as it had come in, the storm passed, and she regained composure.

"But you do not come here to talk about décor, do you? You come to talk about Fronsac."

"He was your lover." It was a statement not a question.

"He was," she confirmed. "Congratulations." She spoke with great sarcasm punctuated by a clap of her hands. "You found out the great secret of me. The mayor's wife and a penniless artist, oh, what a scandal it would be! Are you going to tell anyone?" Her tone was ironic, but her face betrayed a hint of anxiety.

"No," Shaefer told her, and she slumped in relief, "unless it has anything to do with the deaths of Bill Holbrook or Georges Fronsac."

"It doesn't. You have my word on that. I barely knew Bill and had no reason to kill him. Obviously, I knew Georges quite well, but I didn't kill him. Why would I? He was the only thing in this place saving me from death by boredom." Her anger was unfeigned.

"Perhaps he threatened to tell people about the affair."

"Georges?" she cried out in disbelief. "Never. He

was a true gentleman," she said without a hint of irony. "The very soul of discretion."

"Even if that were so, you might have been jealous of him. Or perhaps he tried to end it with you."

She smiled bitterly. "And who was there to have been jealous of? You think he could have found anyone else to compare to me in a small town like this? Bah! And even if he had wanted to end it with me—and he did not—I would not have killed him for it. Believe me, monsieur, I have too much sense for that. I have no desire to be shut up in that miserable little prison."

"I see," Shaefer replied carefully. "And what about Monsieur Farigoule?"

"What about him?"

"Could he have known about the affair?"

Angelique Farigoule didn't even blink.

"No," she said flatly. "My husband had no idea. So, he had no reason to kill Fronsac either. And even if he had known, I doubt he would have killed because of it. He is not the type."

"You'd be surprised how many people who aren't the type to commit murder have, in fact, committed murder," Shaefer observed.

"Not Henri. Un crime passionnel? Him?" Her voice dripped scorn. "Jamais! It is not blood that flows through his veins, but ice water and ink. Oh, he might kill for a profit or for a political office, but he would never take such a risk for me!" She clearly believed what she was saying. That didn't, however, necessarily make her right. "Besides," she added, "he was home that night."

"And he didn't go out once?"

"Non," she replied. "I was here all night, and I would have known if he'd left. Oh, it might be better for me if my husband were a murderer. The guillotine could then make me a free woman. But sadly, it is not so." She certainly seemed mournful enough about the possibility, but Shaefer could not dismiss the possibility she might be covering for her husband. Or possibly for herself.

"If you don't mind my asking, why exactly did you marry Monsieur Farigoule in the first place?"

"For money, of course," she answered blandly. "And for position. When Papa died, I learned he left me little but debts. I was terrified of what would happen to me. I do not know which I feared worse—starving on the streets or having to work in some dreary office or shop." She gave a cynical grimace. "Then Henri showed up asking for my hand, offering me a comfortable life as wife of the mayor." Her words dripped irony. "And fool that I was, I accepted him. People always talk about how pleasant it is living in the country. Let me tell you it is pleasant for at most a month before you want to tear off your clothes and run around screaming. At least if I had taken a boring job in an office or a shop, I could have stayed in Marseilles and had my evenings to do what I pleased." The words seemed to spill out of her, like water boiling over from a pot on the stove. Shaefer didn't dare interrupt her but let her vent like steam from a kettle. "This house, monsieur, may be more comfortable than the town prison, but it is no less confining. My sittings with Georges were the only times since I came here I ever felt truly free." A wistfulness entered her expression, and she was finally silent.

"When did it begin with the two of you?" Shaefer asked her.

"This summer. Sometimes I'd get so sick of being cooped up in this tomb, I like to walk in the woods. He liked walking out there himself. One day, we find each other. We had met before, of course, but never alone."

"He suggested painting a portrait of you to your husband, didn't he?"

"Oui. And Henri refused. God forbid anyone pay more attention to me than to him! But summer when we meet out in the woods we talk, and I tell him if he still want to draw me, I'd like to pose for him. So, I start meeting him in his little cottage to pose. But it get very hot, no? So, it easier for me to pose au naturel!" She looked at Shaefer with an expression of defiance, but he didn't react. "Besides, as Fronsac tell me, it only right to make a record of my fine little body when I am still in my prime!" She smiled at the memory. "Now he was a man I could think might commit un crime passionnel. Artists—they have fire in them, do they not?"

"And you saw such a fire in Fronsac?" Shaefer said with some surprise. "He seemed fairly quiet to me."

She shook her head and pursed her lips. "Seemed quiet," she repeated. "Seemed."

"But, as the English say, still waters ran deep, eh?"

"Oui. Oh he had depths that one. When we made love, he was like a beast. Tireless!" She gave a sigh of adulation, then a shadow came over her face. "But it was not just that. There was something else too. Something in his past that troubled him. I could see it, even though he never tell me. I ask him many times, but he said I was better off not knowing. That the guilt was his to bear alone."

"Guilt? He actually said guilt?"

"Oui. A great sin he called it. But I do not think he told anyone about it except maybe the priest!"

"Which does me no good, since priests never break the seal of confession even to stop killers," Shaefer thought aloud. "Lord knows we tried plenty of times back in Germany!" He shook his head. "I have always found it an odd religious practice myself."

"Do not let the other people of Munier hear you say that," Angelique told him with a cynical look. "It wasn't so very long ago around here they burned members of your race at the stake."

"And they sent Dreyfus to Devil's Island," Shaefer muttered almost to himself. "No, I do not intend to stay in France any longer than absolutely necessary," he confided. "Which is why any information you can offer me about Fronsac or Bill Holbrook would be much appreciated. I understand you met the latter as well?"

"But of course. The American gentleman was most friendly," she emphasized with some irony. "Perhaps he hoped he could tempt me to be his mistress. And perhaps I would have if I had not already found Fronsac. But as it was, a girl hardly needs two lovers and a husband, does she? And I had no wish to trade Fronsac for another. He was not only skilled in les arts de la chambre but quite discreet. Americans like Monsieur Holbrook do not know how to be discreet. They are too loud. Fronsac thought so too. Always he complain how Holbrook talk too much, drink too much, always putting on a big show."

"And yet he and Holbrook were old friends?" Shaefer wondered. "It was Fronsac who got Madame Dellaire to invite Holbrook to the chateau."

"Maybe but he didn't like it so much when Holbrook arrived," Angelique retorted. "He kept saying he hoped Holbrook wouldn't stay for very long. Said it made it harder for him to sleep while he was around."

"Harder to sleep?" Shaefer echoed sharply. "Are you sure?"

"Oui." She cocked her head to the side and frowned. "It almost like having Holbrook around made him nervous. I do not think he wanted to invite Holbrook down here at all, but the man insisted, and Fronsac did not know how to tell him no."

"Or couldn't tell him no," Shaefer suggested. "Is it possible Holbrook had something on Fronsac? That he knew some secret of Fronsac's that he held over his head?"

Angelique looked surprised, then thoughtful. "Perhaps. Perhaps whatever it was that troubled Fronsac was Holbrook's...how you say...leverage over him. That would explain some things, yes. Like why Fronsac seem almost relieved when Holbrook died. Though he did feel sorry for Mademoiselle West. You know for a while I feel jealousy of Mademoiselle West.

Not just because Fronsac like her, but because she is so free. She has her own money and no husband. That is the best thing for a woman. I am sure Madame Dellaire would agree."

This was not a matter Shaefer felt himself qualified to weigh in on and so he remained silent. He did reflect on how much Angelique's sentiments echoed those of Mary Grey.

"Do you have any more questions for me?" Angelique asked. "Or I may be at peace?"

"Just one last thing. I heard Fronsac sold his work to dealers in Avignon and Marseilles. Do you know who any of them were?"

She blinked. "Maybe he mention a couple names," she said slowly.

"Can you write them down for me?" Shaefer requested. "I'd like to contact them."

"Very well." Angelique produced pen and paper from one of the desks and wrote down two names and one address. "I know Monsieur Houdin's address because I've been to his shop in Marseilles," she explained. "But Monsieur Perigot of Avignon I only know by name."

"I am sure I can find him. Merci." Shaefer tipped his hat and bid her farewell.

As he walked down the grand stairs, he was

greeted by Mayor Henri Farigoule himself, who got straight to the point.

"I understand you've been talking to my wife, without my permission."

"That is not illegal, is it?" Shaefer asked with wide-eyed innocence.

"Why did you wish to speak to Madame Angelique?" the mayor demanded.

"I asked her about Bill Holbrook," Shaefer told him truthfully. "But she didn't know much about him."

"You came here just for that?" The mayor looked suspicious. "How long have you been talking to her?"

"I haven't checked my watch."

"Do not be impertinent with me!" His eyes narrowed into slits. "You know we do not favor your kind here in Munier."

"By my kind, do you mean Germans or Jews?"

"Pick one," he snapped. "I assure you, if you persist in your campaign of harassing the town's citizens you will be made to feel most unwelcome."

Shaefer had never felt particularly welcome in Munier to begin with, but he knew all too well that with the likes of Farigoule as an enemy, things could get far, far worse. He did his best to maintain his composure.

"Since I cannot expect the pleasure of your

hospitality," he said cheerfully, "I will show myself out. Oh, but I must collect my driver as well."

"He'll be sent out to you!"

Moments later, Shaefer was cooling his heels by the Peugeot only to witness Raoul be unceremoniously shoved out of the back entryway. As the door closed behind him, Raoul let out a long string of French words Shaefer didn't recognize but correctly guessed were all swear words.

"For a politician, he's not a very gracious host, is he?" Shaefer observed.

"Never have I seen such rudeness before," Raoul fumed. "Not even in Paris! I wish he had killed Fronsac so we might get to see him in handcuffs."

"You say 'wish' not 'hope' as if you know he didn't do it?"

"He couldn't have," Raoul stated glumly. "Both he and Madame Angelique were home all that night. The cook, butler, and maid all swore to it."

"You questioned all of them? How diligent of you." Shaefer nodded in appreciation. "No wonder Jorisse recruited you for spy duty."

"I'm not a spy—" Raoul began indignantly.

"It was a compliment not an insult."

"Oh."

Raoul looked surprised and mollified as Shaefer continued to speak. "Also, if it's any consolation, Mayor Farigoule is not entirely out of the clear for Fronsac's murder. Even if he didn't do the deed himself, it's always possible he hired someone to do it for him." Raoul began looking excited, and Shaefer hastened to dampen his ardor. "I said possible, not probable. Fronsac's murder was hardly the work of a professional hitman."

"How can you be so sure?" Raoul demanded.

"Because they don't use corkscrews," Shaefer answered him simply.

"Oh." Raoul's body sagged in disappointment. "I guess they don't."

"Yet," Shaefer said, and the word buoyed Raoul's hopes. "It is still just within the realm of possibility that Farigoule paid a relative amateur of a thug to do the deed."

"I could ask around," Raoul spoke eagerly. "Find out if there's anyone Farigoule has to dirty his hands for him. Plenty of poachers around here who could have done the deed. You kill enough creatures hunting, it is not such a big difference to move from slaughtering something with four legs to something with two, non?"

"Perhaps not," Shaefer said after a moment's deliberation. "Though you'd think a poacher would have simply shot him."

"Maybe he was worried about the sound of the gun?" Raoul was not ready to give up his theory just yet.

"Maybe, but then why not use your own hunting knife?" Shaefer frowned. "But for the moment, let us put that aside."

Raoul most expressly did not want to put the matter aside and was wondering how to voice such objections without seeming too impertinent, but Shaefer's next words changed his mind.

"I need you to get the car ready for a trip to Avignon. And Marseilles as well."

"At once, monsieur!" Raoul took off to the Peugeot whistling a tune from *La Vie Parisienne.*

CHAPTER FIFTEEN

Upon arrival in Paris, Mary's first instinct was to contact Jorisse and get straight to work. Harriet, however, proclaimed they were both in dire need of a change of clothes and a hot bath.

"Who would even speak to us?" Harriet argued. "We look like common street trash. And this is Paris. They always judge you by your wardrobe."

Mary wasn't sure she completely agreed with this reasoning, but in the afterglow of the night before, she let Harriet talk her into a shopping expedition. It was a decision she soon came to regret. Parisian saleswomen were every bit as snobby and unfriendly as Mary Grey had feared they would be. Or at least Mademoiselles Clarice and Simone were. The two women had matching bobs of sleek dark hair, red lipstick, and chic little black dresses which made them appear so much alike Mary innocently asked if they were sisters. They were not, and they seemed offended by the question. In fact, they seemed to find everything about their English customers offensive. Clarice and Simone each had a way of wrinkling their noses and shaking their heads that was far more expressive than mere words on their opinion of waiting on two rumpled, uncouth foreigners still recovering from a nearly sleepless night. Fortunately, the first stop Harriet and Mary made that morning was to a bank to collect a pile of French banknotes, for it was only the sight of the cold hard cash that kept them from being thrown out at once. As it was, while Clarice and Simone did condescend to take Harriet's money in exchange for merchandise, they managed to make it overwhelmingly clear what an impossible imposition it was to do so. Their attitude was akin to that of an impoverished aristocrat forced to sell their beloved ancestral home to vulgarians.

"No wonder everyone calls the Frogs rude," Mary grumbled after they finally left the store, bags in hand.

"Even by French standards, that was pretty awful.

I should have taken a harder stance with the two of them. That kind of woman will always walk all over you if you're not firm."

"French women?"

"Women who work in high end stores," Harriet responded grimly. "I don't know why, but somehow such places always seem to attract the worst sort of girl. They make East End street walkers look tame and civilized in comparison."

"Perhaps they start out normal," Mary speculated, "but the combination of perfume smells and the sound of the cash register poisons their brain."

"Maybe," Harriet agreed amiably, and they shared a good laugh before finding a small hotel. After booking a pair of separate but adjoining rooms for the sake of appearances, they called Jorisse from the front desk phone and arranged to meet him at a nearby café in an hour's time. This gave them ample time to shower, change, and get their morning coffee in before the lawyer arrived.

*

"Bonjour, mesdames! Good to see you again, Mademoiselle West," Jorisse greeted her warmly, pecking both her cheeks. "I must say you are looking wonderful," he declared in admiration.

"Freedom suits me, I believe," Harriet quipped.

"It most certainly does," he enthused and added as a clear afterthought, "And you look well too, Miss Grey."

"Thanks," she answered in a voice as dry as corn meal. "I'm flattered!"

"Where is Monsieur Shaefer, by the way? And Raoul? And my car?"

"We left them behind," Harriet confessed. "Shaefer still has avenues to follow up in Provence."

"And you left my car and driver with him?" Jorisse blurted out.

"Paris has the Métro and taxis," Harriet responded airily. "So Shaefer needed the car more."

"Perhaps he did," Jorisse replied icily. "But I would appreciate it if you didn't dispose of my property and my servants so cavalierly on my behalf!"

"And I'd appreciate it if you didn't sic an English-speaking chauffeur on my friends to spy on them," Harriet tartly retorted. "But I suppose neither one of us is perfectly content then, are we?"

She and Jorisse exchanged a pair of glares.

"Why did you ask for this appointment?" he demanded. "Was it to finally inform me of the new arrangements?" His voice dripped sarcasm.

"Not exactly," Mary confessed.

"Oh?" Jorisse cocked his head in an expectant fashion.

"Truth is, we need your help."

"But of course," Jorisse muttered, rolling his eyes to the sky as if to ask why the Good Lord couldn't send him less difficult clientele. "Tell me everything!"

Mary proceeded to fill him in on every event that had transpired after he left. It was a long story, and as Harriet had heard it before and was sleepy, she inadvertently yawned a couple of times. Jorisse, however, was riveted. At the news of how they'd found Fronsac's corpse, he shuddered and mentally congratulated himself once more on his prompt return to Paris. Discretion was truly the better part of valor. He listened with interest as to the discovery of Fronsac's probable mistress and all the other village gossip.

"So, you see," Mary concluded, "we really need to find out everything we can about Holbrook and Fronsac's former lives in Paris."

"As it happens," Jorisse replied, "I've made some inquiries of my own about the late Bill Holbrook." With great fanfare, he pulled out a piece of paper from his pocket. "The name and addresses for his old landlady, his past employer, and his personal tailor!" he proclaimed proudly.

Mary mumbled a thank-you as she grabbed the paper, before asking, "But what about Georges Fronsac?"

"I don't have anything on Fronsac," Jorisse answered. "How could I? No one told me I was to investigate him."

"That's true," Mary admitted. "But now that you do know, anything you could find out would be most helpful."

"I'll get right on it," Jorisse proclaimed. His earlier irritation about Shaefer retaining the car had now given way to interest in the current matter. This was the sort of detective work he liked: sitting in his comfortable office and making calls, rather than walking across muddy fields or tripping over dead bodies. He bid them adieu with a cheerful wave.

Their first stop was Holbrook's former apartment in the Latin Quarter which they took a taxi to. On the ride over, Mary marveled at how even the shabbier neighborhoods in Paris somehow had a beauty and charm one could not find in London. Street musicians performed on every corner, and every woman in the street looked... Well, she shopped in Paris. But pretty as it all was, there were still beggars everywhere sleeping on benches and doorsteps. Nor was there anything pretty about the sanitation truck which rolled down the street emitting an odor that could make a water buffalo gag.

The driver let them off in front of a building more dilapidated than its neighbors. This, it seemed, was the former address of Bill Holbrook.

"Ugh," Harriet muttered, examining the peeling mustard paint and cracked concrete steps. "No wonder Bill stayed so long in the country! Can you imagine living like this?"

"Actually, I can," Mary told her coolly, and Harriet flushed.

"Sorry—I just... Well, I forget. I never mean anything by it."

"I know you don't," Mary told her, and it was true. Harriet didn't mean anything by it. It wasn't her fault she'd been raised in the lap of luxury and had inherited great wealth. She was never haughty or mean about it. But it was a gap between her and Mary, nevertheless.

"Let's go find the landlady," Mary suggested.

Madame Thierry was skin wrapped around bones with a thick gray bun on her prominent skull.

"Why are you asking about Holbrook?" she asked Mary suspiciously. "You're not with the police. Are you reporters?"

"We're not," Harriet cut in. "But I was there when

he died, and I have some questions."

"Hmmmm," the old lady muttered and gave Harriet a careful once-over, noting the fine clothes and expensive shoes. She then examined Mary as well. While not as fashionable as Harriet, she still passed muster.

"Ask your questions," Madame Thierry offered, and Harriet gave Mary a smug look as if to say, "See? Clothes do make the difference here!" Mary acknowledged it with a nod. This time at least, Harriet had been right.

Disappointingly, Madame Thierry had little to offer in the way of solid information. News of Holbrook's death had caused her no particular grief, and she had already found a new tenant for the American's rooms: a student at the Pasteur Institute. Monsieur Holbrook was known to stay out late regularly and come home inebriated but that was true for at least half her lodgers, and she was fortunately a sound sleeper. So long as he didn't damage anything and paid his rent on time she did not mind. She claimed to have no knowledge of Holbrook's personal life or social circle. "I make a point of not spying on my tenants—especially the single gentleman," she informed Harriet in French. "The less attention I pay them the happier we all are." Then she added with a glint of peasant shrewdness, "Would you want a landlady who pried into your business?"

Mary had to admit she'd prefer one who didn't but noted in England you often didn't get a choice in the matter.

"Well, here in France," Madame Thierry said haughtily, "we know the value of privacy."

Further questioning revealed Madame Thierry had also already boxed up all his belongings but, without any express wishes from family members to forward his things, was at an impasse. Should she try to sell them? Give them away to the Good Sisters? Or just throw them out altogether? She had no problem whatsoever letting Harriet and Mary take a look.

As it turned out, there wasn't much to look at; most of Holbrook's personal effects had gone with him to the chateau and what was left were bathing trunks for summer, some heavy coats for winter, a pile of books, and a folder of personal documents including his birth certificate, a receipt from a Parisian hospital, and immigration papers. There was a dusty old manuscript that appeared to have been Holbrook's attempt at a novel— and a pile of rejection letters as well. They also found an envelope of what looked like family photographs which Harriet confiscated.

"I'll see to it these get sent back to his family," she

declared.

They left Bill Holbrook's lodgings feeling little wiser than when they had arrived.

"You'd have thought we'd have found at least one clue," Harriet complained.

"Perhaps we did, and we don't know it yet," Mary reasoned. "You never know what may or may not prove useful later on. That's why I write everything down."

"Still seems pretty boring," Harriet grumbled. "Going through piles and piles of papers."

"Well, it's better than when things get exciting," Mary philosophized. "What with people bringing out weapons and all." It was a casual quip, but it got Harriet's attention.

"So that's what your work is? Boring slogs through paperwork broken up by the occasional confrontation with violent criminals?"

"That's oversimplifying it a bit," Mary responded with dignity. "But yes. I suppose you could call it that."

"Sounds a lot like a career in the Army," Harriet mused. "You're something of a soldier then, aren't you?"

"I never thought of it that way before, but I suppose I am," Mary answered.

"I can't say I ever saw myself as a soldier's bride," Harriet told her frankly. "It might take a while to get used to the idea!"

As they left the boarding house, a pair of gen-darmes passed them by, and Harriet instinctively averted her eyes.

"Cheer up. They're not trying to arrest you like Bruno," Mary told her.

"They might if they knew I'm technically on the run from Munier," Harriet replied grimly. "For now, let's just try to avoid policemen, shall we?"

*

The newspaper office Holbrook had written for lay in a ten-story building in Central Paris, a place perfumed with the smell of ink and constantly punctuated by the sound of typewriters. They had walked in at a time of chaos with copy boys careening around desks and mul-tiple phones ringing all at once. Eventually Mary physi-cally grabbed a harassed-looking editor who appeared to have slept in the clothes he was wearing in an attempt to get someone to answer their questions. Yes, he knew who Holbrook was, but he hadn't worked very closely with the man.

"Can you direct us to someone who did?" Mary asked with evident exasperation.

"Richard Nolan and Henry Lomax," the editor

promptly replied. "They hung out with him the most."

"Where are their desks?" Mary demanded.

The editor pointed to a pair of desks containing multitudes of papers but no human occupants, and Mary cursed silently under her breath until he added, "You'll probably find them down at Emile's."

"Emile's?"

"Bar down the block. Any given day, you'll find at least half our reporters there."

*

To enter Emile's was to be immediately enveloped in a thick haze of tobacco smoke and alcohol fumes. Once your eyes adjusted you would see yourself to be in a room of worn leather and wood furnishings with a long mirror, filled almost entirely with men. On the walls in lieu of pictures hung framed newspaper articles and fly-ers, some quite yellow with age. The headlines written in English and French told a local history. Beginning with the Third Republic and Paris Commune, through La Belle Époque, the Great War, the creation of the Maginot Line, and Léon Blum's career. One of the most recent postings was an opinion piece on growing tensions with Germany and the need for appeasement to avoid war. Mary thought to herself it was a good thing Shaefer wasn't there to see it. It would have put him in a foul mood for the rest of the day.

Much to Harriet's surprise, Mary went over to the bar, found a spoon, and started clinking a glass until the room quieted down.

Still, for the first time since she'd come to France, Mary could hear voices speaking English in the background. Admittedly they had American rather than British accents, but she could understand what they were saying. Bits and pieces of conversation reached her ear.

"Police in Danzig are now seizing Jewish assets."

"Checked out the new Hemingway yet? He can write, that cocky bastard!"

"The whole Nine-Power Treaty conference between Japan and China is a joke. Why the hell would Japan concede anything now when they're winning?"

Between that and the copious amounts of beer being served, it felt a bit like being in an English pub, and that put Mary at ease.

"Richard Nolan and Henry Lomax," she called out. "Are either of you present?"

One hand went up, then another. One of the two was a slim man with eyes the same gray as his suit and a face that looked like it had been carved with a hatchet. The other, in contrast, was a stocky sort of fellow with horn-rimmed glasses.

"Would you be willing to talk about Bill Holbrook?" Mary asked simply.

"Sure," the hatchet-faced man replied. "If you'll get the next round of drinks."

"Done!" Harriet agreed. They found a cramped booth in the back where they all crowded in together.

Introductions were made; the slim, hatchet-faced man was Richard Nolan and Stocky Spectacles was Henry Lomax. Both of them, in the grand old fashion of newsies, put in orders for beer and Mary happily joined them.

"What happened to no drinking on the job?" Harriet teased.

"Just trying to fit in," Mary answered breezily.

"Guess I'll have one too then. Make that four beers for the table," Harriet informed the young waiter who vanished and returned in a flash with four glasses and four bottles of Pelforth. After an obligatory round in honor of the late Mr. Holbrook, they got down to business. Richard, Henry, and Bill all went way back. Bill had in their opinion been a pretty good writer.

"His stuff was always zippy," Henry noted.

"Though not exactly hard-hitting," Richard noted. "Bill didn't go for serious assignments. More lifestyle pieces and other filler." There was a hint of disapproval in his voice that Henry seemed to catch.

"Come on, Dick," Henry wheedled. "We've been over this before. Features and filler are the stuff that helps sell papers in the first place. We've all had to write some. Even me. Even you!"

"Yeah, but you and I write serious stuff too. Bill never did," Richard retorted. "I wouldn't have minded so much if he hadn't had talent, but he did. Seemed like a waste." He shook his head at the folly of it. "I was always telling him, go for a bigger story. Politics, crime, social issues, that kind of thing. But politics bored him, social issues depressed him, and crime scared him."

"He couldn't stand the sight of blood," Harriet recalled.

"He was an 'eat, drink, and be merry' kind of guy," Henry said with a sad half smile. "Wanted to enjoy life to the fullest. Even now, seems strange to think of him dead."

"It is," Harriet agreed with a certain melancholy. She had not loved Bill Holbrook, but she had liked him well enough, and it was indeed a shame he had died. Particularly under the circumstances he had.

"Yeah, well if you ask me, he could take the 'drink and be merry' part too far," Richard opined. "Remember the accident?"

Harry let out a whoosh of breath in response.

"What accident?" Harriet wondered.

"About eighteen months ago, Bill was in a car crash," Richard explained.

"That's right," Mary remembered. "At the autopsy they discovered some old injuries to his shoulder and ribs."

Richard nodded. "When he first got to Paris, Bill bought this old Charron car for a song, after the original owner died. You ask me, the thing belonged on the scrap heap instead of the road, but Bill loved it anyway."

"I know the type," Mary commented, thinking of Shaefer's attachment to the Aeroford he'd left back in England.

"Bill loved to take that car out full throttle whenever he could," Richard continued. "Especially after he'd had a few drinks. I used to tell him he needed to slow down but he just laughed. And then one day, sure enough he goes and totals the damn thing! Probably because he was drunk as a skunk." He looked disgusted but also vaguely satisfied.

"We don't know that, Dick," Henry admonished.

"Sure we don't, Henry." Richard gave his naïve friend a vaguely pitying look, but Henry stayed firm.

"We don't! Bill said it wasn't even him driving the car, but the other guy."

"What other guy?" Mary broke in sharply.

"Some painter friend of Bill's," Henry answered.

"I don't know if he was a friend so much as an acquaintance," Richard spoke up. "Bill used him as a source whenever he was writing anything about the art world in town." He frowned. "What was his name anyway? Ferrier? Fromage?"

"Fronsac." Harriet and Mary spoke at once.

"That was it!" Richard snapped his fingers. "Fronsac. Wait, how did you know?" He frowned.

"He was murdered in Munier. Only days after Bill Holbrook was poisoned."

Mary's words had an immediate effect on both men. Henry let out a whoosh of breath as Richard got a gleam in his eye. A gleam any fellow reporter could recognize as the sight of a newsie who's caught the scent of a particularly juicy story. Mary had the sinking feeling in her stomach she had made a grave mistake.

"You don't say?" Richard said. "Well, well, well!" He drained his glass, then pulled out a pen and notepad. "Who did you say you ladies were again?"

Chapter Sixteen

Raoul quite enjoyed driving Shaefer to Avignon. As it happened, their route took them quite near Raoul's home village, and he mentioned this to his passenger with perhaps some hopes of making a detour. Alas it was not to be. Sympathetic as Shaefer was to the urge to catch up with family, there was only so much time in the day, and there was a killer on the loose, perhaps planning another murder already. He nixed Raoul's hopes but suggested by way of consolation that perhaps they could make the trip after the killer's apprehension.

Situated on a bend of the Rhone river, Avignon looked like an illustration from one of Perrault's fairy tales. Built centuries before the birth of Christ, the city had been declared the papal capital by Pope Clement V in 1309. A palace for the popes was built, then another. The two palaces, old and new, were joined into a splendid residence that was the most fortified such palace of its time. Seven popes reigned from within the palace's walls, and for nearly a century, Avignon was the undisputed capital of Christianity. The papal library of Avignon was the largest in Europe with over two thousand volumes, and the city was a center for commerce and culture alike.

In terms of actual importance, Avignon had by then made a significant comedown, but the city still retained all its beauty. Shaefer, beholding the Gothic buildings and wrecked Saint-Bénézet Bridge, which, at a half mile long, remained magnificent in its decay, was duly impressed. Any other time, he would have enjoyed a chance to play tourist in this monument to medieval times. But again, it was not meant to be. They stopped for directions, then the Peugeot made its way to the Street of the Golden Scissors, and there, flanked by two oak trees, was a little art gallery that had done business with one Georges Fronsac.

As part of reconciling Raoul to not being allowed a home visit, Shaefer left him to enjoy a cigarette on his own. The gallery was a sparkling clean, surprisingly spacious set of rooms furnished with comfortable seating. There was an array of paintings in various styles on the walls and even a few statues on display as well. Even to Shaefer's untrained eye there was some promising work there, and, on another occasion, he might have liked to look around a bit. The first person he saw was a small vivacious young woman wearing a red-and-black shawl embroidered in an Oriental pattern and a red beret to match.

"Bonjour," Shaefer offered awkwardly.

"Bonjour," the girl replied with a cheerful smile.

"Do you speak English?" Shaefer asked hopefully.

"I do," she replied before asking in perfect German, "but wouldn't you prefer to converse in your native tongue?"

"Danke!" Shaefer exclaimed as he went on to enjoy a blissful conversation in his beloved Deutsch. The girl was named Pierrette, and she had studied at university in Paris.

"How did you come to be here?" Shaefer wondered. She gave a rueful smile.

"Ah, Paris! Such a wonderful city but so expensive. And the competition for positions at the big galleries there is quite brutal. Here it is cheaper and more peaceful but still a good art scene. And we have all the conveniences of a proper city at hand, without all the noise and pollution," she reported with evident civic pride in her new adopted town. It also gave Shaefer an opening.

"Do you think that is why Georges Fronsac left Paris for Munier? To get away from noise and pollution?"

Her expression turned grave. "Ah, Georges Fronsac!" she sighed. "Such a loss, that. Such a kind and polite man...which is not always the case with painters." Her voice lowered to a confidential whisper. "Truth is, I do not believe Fronsac came to the country just for the fresh air and views. There was some heavy sin upon his soul." She spoke with simple conviction.

"Sin?" Shaefer repeated. "Did he tell you?"

"No, he did not. But every time he came here to Avignon, he stopped at the Avignon Cathedral to pray."

"Perhaps he liked to pray there simply because he liked it there," Shaefer noted. "I haven't gone in, but I drove by, and it appears most beautiful."

"It is!" she agreed. "But I know other people who were in the church once when he was too, and they saw him in the pews looking up at the altar up ahead of him and weeping. Tears and tears pouring from his red eyes as his body shook with the pain of whatever it was he was hiding."

"Shocking." Shaefer didn't have to feign any interest in that.

"Yes, it must have been a great sin indeed," Pierrette intoned. "One that even Confession and Absolution could not relieve the pain of. I can only hope he found peace in death." Beyond that, she could offer no further information or insight into the late Georges Fronsac. She did offer to show Shaefer some works by a promising local painter and suggested they could arrange direct shipping overseas if necessary, at which point Shaefer pleaded the need to be on his way. He found Raoul back at the car and directed him to their next address in Marseilles.

"What about lunch?" Raoul wondered, sounding plaintive. "I saw several places here that look good."

"No. We can find something on the road," Shaefer instructed, and Raoul glumly obeyed.

It was a long drive to Marseilles and neither Raoul nor Shaefer were in a talkative mood. The former was listening to the pangs of his stomach while the latter kept replaying in his mind's eye the scene of Georges Fronsac crying in the cathedral. Why Avignon and not the church in Munier? Had he just found Avignon's grander cathedral more moving than the modest structure of

Munier? Or had he felt easier unburdening his guilt away from the prying eyes of his neighbors? Perhaps a bit of both. In Shaefer's experience, Catholics were a particularly odd subspecies of Gentiles. They adored beauty yet seemed to wallow in pain.

These musings were interrupted by Raoul finally making a loud and eloquent plea for refreshment or he would drive no farther. They stopped at a cheap roadside tavern before proceeding on to Marseilles.

After the serene beauty of Avignon, Shaefer found Marseilles to be a rude letdown. Almost as large as Paris, it had all the traffic congestion and seedy side streets of its more famous neighbor without any of the famous Parisian charm. True, there was an abundance of classical ruins from its days of Roman occupation, but it seemed spoiled by lying alongside the uglier modern buildings. There was a general gaudiness about the place; a gauche quality that suggested a fundamental vulgarity in the city's character. A result perhaps of its countless centuries as a port of harbor for persons of shady character from all over the world.

The people on the streets were noisy as parrots and all in seeming competition to shove elbows into one another's ribs. They drove past a cinema advertising a showing of *La Dame de Malacca,* and Raoul sighed. He had been meaning to see that film, being a fan of the lovely Edwige Feullière. He reminded himself to demand some time off after his Provence sojourn to catch up with simple pleasures. Really, he had gone above and beyond the chauffeur call of duty here!

Shaefer did not see the movie display because he was distracted by the sight of posters along the side of a building on the opposite street. They were from Parti Socialiste National which needed no translation. And even without reading the words, their meaning would have been evident from the picture of a youth in Nazi uniform wielding a two-headed ax over the heads of a crowd of brutes with exceptionally long noses. Shaefer had seen far too many such signs before, and it was enough to turn his stomach. It also provoked his most fevered imaginings. How many of the seemingly ordinary persons he saw on the streets of Marseilles agreed with the sentiments of the poster? Who among them were sympathetic to the Nazi cause? It was a question he lately found himself asking more and more in all kinds of settings. Was that dignified silver-haired grandmother a Fascist sympathizer? What about the street musician in the bright-blue pants playing the accordion? Or that handsome young man there walking hand in hand with a pretty curly-haired girl. Could one of them have put up the poster? Or both of them together? Had they perhaps first become acquainted at a National Socialist meeting? Shaefer pressed his fingers to his temples as he attempted with all his might to return his brain to the task at hand.

The address listed was on a dingy little street two doors down from a burlesque theatre and right across the street from an unmarked building which Shaefer's police instincts instantly identified as a likely bordello. It was an unmarked three-story building with a worn shingle roof and no signs of habitation.

"Are you sure this is the right place?" Raoul questioned Shaefer.

"No, but it is the only address I have in this town. Let me go in." He tried the buzzer, then found the door itself unlocked, allowing him to go right in. The so-called gallery consisted of a dimly lit hole stuffed full of framed canvasses. It was manned by an oily-looking gentleman named Claude. A few questions quickly revealed Claude could offer no new information on Fronsac. The latter had sold him paintings, yes, but he had never taken Claude into his confidence or even so much as shared a drink with him. Another man might have been insulted by that attitude, but Claude was used to the artistic temperament.

"How long were you planning to stay in Marseilles?" Claude asked of Shaefer.

"Just passing through," Shaefer replied tersely.

"A pity. There is so much in this city to enjoy. If, for instance, you were to spend even a single night here, I could recommend to you where to dine, where to book a hotel, the evening's entertainment," he rattled off blithely. For Claude had met a lot of tourists to his town over the years and was always happy to assist them.

"Thank you, but I really cannot—" Shaefer began.

"Indeed, monsieur." Claude coughed delicately. "If you felt the need for a guide of sorts, I could find you that too. I know a number of lovely local girls who would be willing to show you around." He smiled. Time and experience had taught Claude that while one could make a living acting as a go-between for artists and buyers, acting as a go-between for other services was an excellent supplement. Men with money for paintings were often men in the market for discreet companionship as well. And he knew many professional artists' models willing to provide such additional service.

"No, thank you!" Shaefer quickly answered once the offer was made. Small wonder, he thought, Fronsac had always kept his visits to this particular dealer so short. Shaefer was in such a hurry to get out that he tripped over one painting, and he had to pick it up to check for damage. It was a remarkably vivid Impressionist-style watercolor of the Port of Marseilles and was thankfully unharmed since it looked—and indeed was—expensive. Whatever else could be said about Claude's morals, he did have an eye for picking up good pieces.

"Ah, you have found one of Charles Camoin's works," the oily gentleman proclaimed. "One of Marseilles' most talented sons. Might you be interested..."

"No." Shaefer adamantly refused, though with a tinge of regret. Truthfully it was perhaps the best piece of art he'd seen all day. But that only meant it was more likely to be costly, and he could not call it a business expense. Besides, where in his apartment could he possibly hang it? "I must be on my way," he told Claude with a surprisingly sincere note of regret.

Raoul was surprised to have Shaefer leave the shop so quickly after entering but, looking at his German passenger's scowl, decided not to make a fuss about it. Shaefer's mood was not improved when the traffic leaving Marseilles proved to be even worse than entering it had been. He felt that the entire day had been a waste of gasoline and, more importantly, time. He could only hope things were more fruitful for Mary in Paris.

As the Peugeot finally exited the city, Raoul made

a suggestion.

"You know, it is very late, monsieur. Indeed, it will soon be dark, and we have spent much of the day in the car. Perhaps we should find a place to stop for the night and return to Munier in the morning?" It really had been an inordinate amount of driving for him that day, and he could do with some rest.

Shaefer briefly considered this suggestion. Like Raoul, he was wearied by the day's travels. The idea of retiring early was certainly tempting one, yet... "I'm afraid not," he pronounced finally, much to Raoul's disappointment. "It's best to drive straight through to Munier tonight. We've spent too much time away as it is. For all we know, there's already been a third murder. If it's any consolation," he offered mercifully, "I promise to let you sleep in tomorrow morning. Now keep your foot on that throttle."

"Oui, monsieur, but we must then make a brief stop." They found a station to supply the Peugeot with gasoline and the passengers with bitter black coffee. Thus refueled, Raoul, in the same gallant spirit of the Knights Templar, drove on despite his weariness into the chill of the night. Unlike the knights of old, though, Raoul had no foreknowledge of the possible dangers that awaited him.

CHAPTER SEVENTEEN

Mary didn't know if all reporters were impossibly pushy or if it was strictly an American phenomenon, but Richard Nolan proved to be a very difficult man to be rid of. Once he learned who Harriet was and how she'd just been released from jail, he was a hound with a bone. Or rather a shark smelling blood in the water. Nothing could shake him from such a prize. He clung to their sides with a dogged determination that it would be he—and he alone—who would get the Big Scoop on this one. And Mary could not deter him merely by being rude.

"You know I can get a photographer over right now and get a few pictures of you ladies for the next edition," Richard suggested heartily. "How about it, huh?"

"I'd rather put a thumbtack through my arm!" Mary snapped back as Harriet tried not to laugh. Richard was unfazed.

"All right, she's out, but how about you, then?" Undaunted, he turned his full attention to Harriet. Frankly, she was the one he was more interested in landing, anyway. Not only was she the true star of the story, but also the more photogenic. He could already imagine how thrilled the editor would be to have a portrait of such a beauty on the cover. "A full spread on you, the wrongfully accused English heiress and your ordeal at the hands of the gendarmes. Might wanna wear your pearls," Nolan suggested, much to Mary's horror. Even worse, Harriet looked like she might actually be considering it, which only inflamed Mary even more.

"No!" she snapped. "Harriet, come on—we have an investigation to conduct."

"Investigation?" Nolan looked keener than ever. "What investigation?"

Mary could have bitten off her own tongue. She also could have bitten off Harriet's when the latter casually announced, "Mary here's a detective. Apprentice detective rather."

"Apprentice detective?" Nolan pursed his lips. "Never heard of that one before."

Mary began pulling Harriet's arm in a desperate attempt to get her to go, but the latter stubbornly stood her ground.

"Ever hear of Franz Shaefer then?" Harriet queried with a coy glance.

"Shaefer...Shaefer..." Nolan repeated. "Wait a minute, isn't there some hotshot German detective named Shaefer?"

"You have heard of him then!" Harriet beamed. The fish had taken the bait, and now it was just time to reel it in.

"Wait, she works for Shaefer?" Nolan cocked his thumb toward Mary, who had begun grinding her teeth.

"She does. In fact, we're both long-time friends of his," Harriet cheerfully informed him. "He and Mary were both instrumental in securing my release."

"My oh my." Stars glittered in Nolan's eyes. "This story just keeps getting better and better!"

"Excuse us one moment," Mary hissed before dragging Harriet away to a private vestibule.

"What the hell are you doing?" she demanded.

"Quid pro quo," Harriet responded demurely. "Isn't that what it's called? He told us about Fronsac being in the car crash with Bill, so we give him information on our end. He could still be useful to us, Mary," she pointed out before Mary could object. "He knows Paris and has sources here. He could be a lot of help really, and all we'd have to do in exchange is give him an interview."

"All right then," Mary conceded. Harriet's logic was infuriatingly good. "But it will be you giving him the interview not me. He's more interested in you anyway," she concluded with relief.

They returned to Nolan's side, and Mary said as little as possible while Harriet turned on the charm. She assured Nolan she'd be delighted to give him an exclusive and a head shot, no problem at all.

"Only do you think you could find out more about Bill's accident for us?" she asked him, batting her eyes. Despite Harriet's considerable wiles, Nolan was not the least bit fooled. He knew she was using him for information and was amused more than offended by it. If anything, helping the two Englishwomen find what they were looking for was likely to be the grist for even more juicy articles in the future, and he would be damned sure he'd get them! And despite Mary's hopes, Nolan had no intent of ignoring Miss Grey either. As Shaefer's apprentice/assistant, she was a potential fountain of information, and his instincts told him she had some stories too. Hell, if he played his cards right on this one, he might even get a chance to question Shaefer himself and what a news coup that would be.

"Sure," Nolan replied with a smile as broad and insincere as Harriet's own. "Let's see what we can turn up about Bill's little fender bender!"

The first step was ascertaining when exactly Bill had had his little fender bender. Nolan and Morris both remembered the event had happened the winter before last, sometime after Christmas but not the exact date.

"Too bad we can't subpoena his medical records," Mary grumbled.

"No, but we can do the next best thing," Nolan announced with a big grin. "Check on his work-related absences."

They returned to the newspaper offices to talk to a harried-looking woman named Gladys. As official record keeper for the paper, Gladys spent a lot of time interacting with reporters. As a direct result, she was actively scanning the classified layouts every day looking for another position. Any other position. God in his infinite wisdom must have created writers for some reason, but Gladys for one couldn't figure out what it was. She greeted a summons from Nolan in particular with skepticism, considering him even worse than the dead Holbrook. She originally looked upon Harriet and Mary with suspicion but was pacified somewhat to learn neither of them were employed in the field of journalism or had any interest in joining it. It took much cajoling on Harriet's part, and the discreet offer of some franc notes, before Gladys was finally convinced to let them take a look at Holbrook's file.

"Here it is," Nolan announced. "January 18th, 1936. Bill called the offices from the American Hospital of Paris, explaining why he'd been gone for two days. Says here he even put one of the doctors on the line to confirm he hadn't just been on a bender but really was in a hospital. I remember." Nolan snapped his fingers. "That's when the editor came in and told everyone the news. So, Harry and I went down to the hospital to visit Bill and saw the painter guy Fronsac there."

"If he'd been in the hospital two days, and the call came on the 18th then the accident must have taken place on January 16th," Mary deduced.

"You know, I've got a source in the local Metropolitan Police who could show us traffic accident reports on that date," Nolan mused.

"No!" Harriet shrilly cried out. "No police!"

Nolan raised an eyebrow.

"We'd rather avoid official involvement for the time being," Mary told him.

"Heh." Nolan eyed them shrewdly. "Is that so? Well then, let's check out the headlines," he suggested. Once more, Gladys was summoned, this time to guide them to where the paper kept its stack of first editions. It took a while of sorting through dusty old newspapers, but eventually they found the paper for January 16th. There was nothing about any traffic accidents on the front pages, which were dominated by the Stavisky trial, France's warning to Germany not to disregard its obligations under the Locarno Treaty, and the news of Italy's victory in the Battle of Ganale Doria. Only on the very last page of the Métro section did they find it; a tiny blurb announcing the death of a young woman the day before in a vehicular accident. The girl was identified as Giselle Chernal, aged nineteen, and she had been employed as a seamstress at a design house known as Mimi Merou's.

"That poor girl," Harriet whispered. "To die so young."

"Do you think it was Bill's car that killed her?" Nolan got the immediate point.

"I can't be sure, but it seems probable." Mary replied. "If Fronsac and Holbrook were both involved in an accident that resulted in someone's death, that would be a motive to kill both of them." She reread the piece and read it again, but to Mary's frustration there was so little information to be gleaned. Clearly the death of young Giselle had caused no disturbance at the time in the City of Lights.

But maybe it had brought about ripples, nearly two years later in Munier.

"We've got to find out everything we can about Giselle Chernal," Mary pronounced. "It says here she worked at this Mimi Merou's—let's start there. Someone may remember her. And let's see if we can get her death certificate as well in case it lists next of kin."

*

Mimi Merou's was a smaller fashion house that specialized primarily in accessories like leather goods, handbags, and, of course, chic silk scarves that were the must-have for any fashionable French girl. It was in the manufacturing of the last that Giselle Chernal, along with over fifty other girls, had been employed. The shop floor was a noisy place where one had to almost scream to be heard over the general din. The forewoman was not pleased to have to deal with the interruption particularly when it became clear none of the foreigners had any attention of buying anything. It was Harriet who coaxed the woman into speaking to them, and Harriet who acted as translator. The forewoman herself barely remembered Giselle. She'd been a quiet girl who'd only worked there a few months.

"Did she have any friends among the other girls here?" Mary asked.

The forewoman thought a moment. "I did see her with Nanette Hugard from time to time. In fact, they say Nanette was nearby when Giselle died." Mary let out a whoosh of breath, and Nolan seemed to salivate.

"We need to speak to Nanette," Harriet insisted.

"Nanette doesn't work here anymore. She quit soon afterward. Foolish girl," the forewoman announced with a scowl.

Once this was explained to the others, Mary swore under her breath while Nolan swore openly.

"Do you have any idea where we can find her?" Harriet followed up.

"Non!" she retorted with a huff. "Why would I?"

They were leaving the building feeling all in a bad humor when they were stopped by a mousy-looking girl Mary recognized from the shop floor.

"You look for Nanette?" she asked them in hesitant English.

"Oui!" Harriet cried out eagerly.

"I hear she now works at Le Club Lune in Montparnasse," she told them.

"I know that place." Nolan snapped his fingers. "From the outside anyway."

"Merci beaucoup!" Harriet thanked her as the girl hurried off to her duties.

"So now if you'd kindly direct us to the Club Lune in Montparnasse," Mary suggested, but Nolan shook his head.

"Thing is, ladies, it's strictly a nightclub. Doors won't even open until ten p.m."

"We have to wait that long?" Mary could have torn out her hair in frustration.

"Paris time. What can you do?" he waxed philosophically.

"Actually, I think this might be a good thing," Harriet spoke up. "I don't know about you, but I'm quite exhausted." She gave a delicate cough with a hint of blush to her cheeks. "I didn't sleep well last night. This gives us plenty of time to go back to the hotel and get some rest before we find this Nanette and get her to give us the goods."

"Assuming she has any goods to give," Mary muttered. "But I see your general reasoning." She smiled ruefully. "I'm pretty worn out myself too!"

Nolan saw the women exchange glances with some hidden meaning and found himself puzzled. Must be an Englishwoman thing, he reasoned.

*

At exactly a quarter to ten that night, a taxi dropped Harriet and Mary off at Club Lune to find Nolan already waiting in line to get in. The club itself was earmarked by a large gaudy lit-up sign of a silver crescent moon. Sitting in the moon as if it were a swing was a girl in a top hat, tuxedo tails, and fishnet stockings instead of trousers, winking saucily at onlookers. At 10:00 p.m. on the dot, the doors opened, and they were ushered inside a space furnished with tables covered in white linen, blue leather booths, and a chandelier. Crescent moon-shaped ashtrays littered all available surfaces, and the smell of expensive tobacco smoke permeated the air along with perfume and spirits. A black jazz band played on stage, led by a singer with a dynamite voice, though they competed to make themselves heard against the sounds of clinking glasses, conversation, and popping corks. It took a few minutes, but Harriet finally managed to attract the bartender's attention. Nanette, it seemed, was one of the cigarette girls who served the club, all of them dressed in the same top hat, tuxedo tails, and fish-net stockings as the girl on the sign. She was a pretty girl with a heart-shaped face and very shapely legs. They took a booth and gestured for Nanette to come visit them.

"Cigarettes?" she asked.

"Non," Harriet told her regretfully. "We need to ask you about a girl you knew when you were a seamstress. Giselle."

At the mention of Giselle, all the color drained from Nanette's face.

"I have to work," she replied curtly. "I cannot talk."

"Yes, you can." Harriet fixed her with a gaze. "Stay and talk to us, and we'll buy ten packets of cigarettes from you and a bottle of the best champagne in the house." Mary's mouth dropped open in surprise, but before she could protest, Harriet continued, "That way you can tell your manager you were just entertaining the whims of some high-paying customers. Now take a seat!"

Nanette did so with some reluctance and the order for champagne was put out. When it came, Harriet poured out a glass for Nanette who drank it down quickly and followed it with another. The bubbly restored color to her cheeks and loosened her tongue.

"Oui, I remember Giselle," she began. "Une telle tragedie! So young. I saw it happen." She looked tearful.

"What? What did you see?" Nolan panted with excitement as his hands drew out his notebook.

"It was late that night. Giselle and I had just left work and we parted ways at the streetlight—she to go left and I to go right. Then out of nowhere a car came racing down the street, faster than the devil itself. It tried to take a turn, but it slid out of control. It crash into Giselle, and she flew over the top of the car and then fell onto the street. She was shattered like a doll. After the car hit Giselle, it plowed into a lamp post. And there it stayed until the police and ambulance came. The ambulance take the men in the car with them—one of them was French like me but the other was American. The ambulance, they try to help Giselle too, but it was already too late. They say she must have died immediately when she was struck." As she spoke, Nanette began clenching and unclenching her fists at the memory. "Afterward I do not like working in that neighborhood anymore. I cannot walk past those streets without thinking of what happened, you know? So, I quit and got a job here."

For a moment, no one spoke as they let the gravity of the tale wash over them. Mary found herself picturing all too well that awful night. It reminded her of another horrific car crash that had taken place in wintertime and had ultimately claimed the life of Harriet's late brother Anthony. Judging from her face, Harriet remembered too.

"Why do you think the car crashed?" Nolan finally asked, looking up from the notepad he'd been furiously scribbling in. "Was it because the driver was going too fast? Or was the driver drunk? Or was it just ice on the street?"

"I think the driver was going too fast for a night when there was ice on the street," Nanette replied after some thought. "Perhaps they were drinking, or perhaps not. I do not know. But they were not careful with their driving. That I do know. And it was Giselle who paid the price." She paused. "Something else too. After the men crashed the car and before the police and ambulance arrived...there was something strange."

"Strange?" Mary and Nolan said in unison.

"The American and Frenchman—they switch places in front seat of the car. The American get out of the driver's seat and move to the passenger's seat while the Frenchman got into the driver's seat. I do not understand why they do that, especially when the American was hurt. Even from across the street I could see he in a lot of pain."

Harriet turned pale, and Mary and Nolan shared a glance. So, Richard's instinct had been right, and it had been Holbrook driving the car that night. Most likely, he'd been intoxicated doing so and thus his eagerness to deny having been at the wheel when Giselle was killed. Why, however, had Fronsac gone along with it? Had Holbrook bribed him or threatened him somehow? Or had Fronsac not wanted to take responsibility for letting an inebriated man drive? Whatever the reason had been, the simple fact was that Bill Holbrook had been directly responsible for the death of a teenage girl and Fronsac had helped him escape all culpability for his actions. It would certainly have been a motive to kill both men.

"Why didn't you tell all this to the police?" Mary demanded.

"I did! I tell the police everything, but they did not believe me. They think I'm just a silly seamstress. Or maybe they did not care." There was an endless well of bitterness in her voice. "A little girl from the country dies in a traffic accident—perhaps that was not dramatic enough for them. Est-ce que tu comprends? But I do write to Giselle's family in the country and tell them the truth."

"When you say the country...do you mean Provence, and somewhere around Munier?" Mary asked breathlessly.

"Oui—how you know Giselle from there?"

"Lucky guess," Nolan cut in. "Who were her family in Munier?"

Nanette told them. And as she did so, Mary felt a cold grasp of fear in her heart.

CHAPTER EIGHTEEN

By the time they approached the village of Munier once more, Raoul and Shaefer had switched places as driver and passenger. This switch had come at Shaefer's insistence as he had become increasingly concerned by the chauffeur's obvious exhaustion.

"It's ridiculous," he finally announced. "I've had a chance to catch naps throughout the day, but you have not. I will take over at the wheel for a while."

Raoul's eyelids felt like lead, yet still he protested. "But monsieur, you do not know the way!"

"Bring out a map then and give me directions," Shaefer bid him, and he complied. Raoul was no sooner seated in the backseat than his head lolled back and he began snoring as Shaefer took off. It was fortunate for Raoul that he was an extremely sound sleeper otherwise he'd have been disturbed on the ride. Shaefer's driving had long been a source of concern for his assistant Mary, and being on the roads after dark in a foreign place only made matters worse. Yes indeed, it was all for the good that Raoul was blissfully unconscious during the whole thing. Finally, their perilous journey came to an end, and Shaefer haphazardly parked the car on the by-now-familiar cobblestone street.

"We're here!" he proclaimed triumphantly to Raoul, whose only response was snores.

"*Raoul!*" Shaefer resorted to shouting, and the chauffeur started wide awake.

"Où sommes-nous?" he cried out.

"The inn at Munier," Shaefer replied. "Let's go and sleep in a real bed."

The two of them poured out of the car and stumbled through the door to find old Gaston in a chair by the fire.

"Vouz êtes en retard," the old man remarked.

"He says we're late," Raoul translated.

"Give him my apologies but remind him we never asked him to wait up for us," Shaefer said. Raoul began to speak, but Gaston waved him off before walking away somewhere in back and returning with two steaming mugs.

"Buvez!" he commanded in a gruff voice as he put the mugs on the table. Raoul eagerly grabbed one and gulped the liquor down. Shaefer didn't pick his drink up but rather rubbed his temples.

"I hope Mary Grey had a more productive day," he thought aloud. "Did she call while we were gone by any chance? Or leave a message?"

Gaston's face remained impassive.

"Raoul, ask him if Miss Grey called!" Shaefer ordered, but Raoul didn't seem to hear him. His eyes once more were closed, and he slumped from his chair onto the floor.

"Raoul!" Shaefer exclaimed and jumped to his side. He checked Raoul's wrist for a pulse and found one; slow but steady. The chauffeur was still alive, but he was now in a very deep sleep indeed.

"She did call," Gaston said. "Miss Grey. She called one of my neighbors and was desperate to speak to you in person. But she refused to give an official message for me to give to you. I think perhaps she doesn't trust me."

"Gottverdammt!" Shaefer swore. "Does everybody in this country lie about speaking English?"

"Not everyone," Gaston intoned. "Just me." He gave a sad smile, and Shaefer's eyes went to the two mugs on the table. One drunk in full by Raoul and one untouched by him.

"Is it fatal?" he asked Gaston.

"Non." The innkeeper shook his head. "Just something to help you sleep. Give me a little more time to figure out what to do. Believe me, monsieur, if I had wanted you or any of your friends dead, they'd be dead! I've had plenty of chances."

"And you've killed before. Twice at least." Shaefer nodded as everything began to fall into place.

"Oui, monsieur. The great detective finally got there!" He smiled. "Though to be fair, why would you ever suspect me at all? No one notices the harmless old man who runs the inn. The American fellow didn't. He never even turned to see who handed him his drink that night. He just swilled it down without a single merci!" Gaston shook his head. "Such a rude boorish fellow, eh?"

"And Fronsac?"

"More polite than Holbrook, but still he had trouble remembering my name when I knocked on his door to talk to him. But he was civil enough to offer me a drink. At first, I thought maybe I could wait until his back was turned and poison his drink. But it just seemed easier to use the corkscrew."

"You used the bicycle, didn't you?" Shaefer's mind flashed back to how tired Gaston had looked the day Fronsac's body was found. "To get all the way to Fronsac's cottage and back."

"Very good! Yes, the bike it is old, and the ride was hard on me at this age, but some things can't be helped. I had to get to him quickly. You were on the chase."

"But why?" Shaefer wanted to keep Gaston talking, but there was real curiosity behind his question as well. "Why kill two men who were practically strangers to you?"

"Because they killed my granddaughter," Gaston answered. "Giselle. She was the last of my bloodline. Everyone else died in the Great War and the influenza that followed. She was all I had left. And they left her to die in the streets like a dog. You know I never wanted Giselle to go to Paris. I told her it wasn't safe. But when a young girl has spent her whole life in the country, she wants to see the big city, you know? But the men who killed her—they went and they left Paris and they both eventually found their way to Munier. Of all the places in the world, they found their way here! A sign from God. I had to take it," he concluded with the absolute certainty of a religious zealot. "It was out of my hands."

"And what now?" Shaefer asked. "Now that your vengeance is complete, what next?"

"I'm not really sure," Gaston admitted. "I hadn't really thought so far ahead." His gaze turned to the dying fire. From somewhere outside, Shaefer could hear footsteps running toward them, but Gaston paid no attention as he continued to speak. "Truth is, I don't have anything left to live for, now do I? But suicide is a sin, so I suppose I must let the laws of man be the one to kill me, eh?"

The door of the inn flew open, revealing a red-faced Inspector Bruno and a shaking Etienne. Both held revolvers in their hands. Etienne trembled with fear, but Bruno was as excited as a child at a carnival. This was the sort of assignment he'd dreamed about when he first joined the police force.

"Now they come," Gaston murmured, looking oddly amused. "C'est la vie!"

"Why are you here?" Shaefer asked Bruno and Etienne with less gratitude than Bruno would have liked.

"Mademoiselle Grey called us directly from Paris," Etienne explained. "She told us Gaston had probably killed both Fronsac and Holbrook and that she feared for your safety."

"Good on her part and for you as well," Shaefer

responded. "But it's really not so dangerous. If the two of you could put away your gu—" To Shaefer's shock and Bruno's glee, Gaston pulled out a pistol from his side pocket.

"Voilà!" Gaston cried out gleefully as he cocked the pistol at the policemen.

"Tire!" Bruno shouted as if he were commanding a regiment at Waterloo.

"No! Don't!" Shaefer screamed but it was too late.

Both Bruno and Etienne fired their weapons at the same time. Etienne's shot fired into the mantelpiece above the old fireplace. Bruno's aim was true; he hit Gaston directly through the heart.

Shaefer rushed to the old man's side to hear his final words.

"Merci, Bruno. Maintenant c'est fini." And he was gone.

Shaefer grabbed the pistol still clutched in Gaston's hand. It was a rusty old thing so ancient it might have served in the Napoleonic wars. The chamber was empty. It had been unloaded.

EPILOGUE

Raoul woke up some hours later with a sore head, but otherwise none the worse for wear. His shock upon learning what had transpired while he was unconscious was a great one, and by way of compensation, Shaefer later let him stay several days with his own family in Provence. Jorisse complained of the inconvenience but was secretly mollified by the relief of having been safely in Paris, away from the excitement and terror of Munier.

Shaefer would always maintain that Gaston had committed suicide by policeman, but officially it was written up as death by misadventure, thus allowing the old innkeeper to be buried in sacred ground. Some may have whispered objections to this, but just like the whisperings following the death of the late Monsieur Dellaire so many years ago, nothing came of it.

In the aftermath of Gaston's death, even Inspector Bruno was willing to admit Harriet's innocence. This did not prevent him from taking offense at the fact she'd defied his orders and left Munier for Paris, but it did deter him from taking any legal action. Being involved in the resolution of a high-profile double homicide brought him attention from his superiors—and a transfer to Strasbourg. It was not Paris, but it was a real city far superior to dull little Munier. And its position on the German border guaranteed it would be a lively posting.

After Bruno's transfer, Constable Etienne was promoted to inspector and had the little station house all to himself. Despite this unexpected rise in his career and the increase in salary and prestige that came with it, he suffered from nightmares for months after the shooting. Slowly with time, however, he recovered as Munier once more returned to its usual sedentary state. And he took comfort in the knowledge that neither he nor the town were likely to ever see such levels of violence and bloodshed again anytime soon.

Madame Dellaire decided she'd had enough of Munier altogether and took up rooms full time in Nice, leaving the running of the chateau and estate to Maxim. For a long time, Maxim was quite lonely. But as luck would have it, come spring a handsome young drifter came around looking for work. He and Maxim Dellaire got on splendidly right from the start. Maxim hired him as an assistant and gave him Fronsac's old cottage to stay in, where Maxim called upon quite regularly.

Richard Nolan got his exclusive interview with Harriet West and another with Franz Shaefer as well, all in a special edition of the paper detailing the sensational story behind Bill Holbrook's death. It was the best-selling edition of the year and Nolan's biggest story yet.

Harriet West returned to London with Franz Shaefer and Mary Grey. She and Mary once more became flatmates, along with Ahab the cat. But while Mary continued working by Shaefer's side, she also began volunteering her services with the London Chapter of the Red Cross. Upon reflection, Harriet decided that she also needed something to busy herself with while Mary was at work. She didn't feel particularly inspired to join a steno pool or take up other paid employment, but there were always plenty of opportunities for charitable and volunteer work. After a great deal of deliberation, Harriet soon started immersing herself in a society devoted to assisting the flood of refugees arriving from Europe.

A joyous event took place in the Farigoule household in the summer of 1939 with the birth of the mayor's firstborn son, Claude. Claude was a source of great pride for his father and the center of his all his mother's affections. He would grow to be a strong handsome child with an unexpected talent for drawing.

About Winnie Frolik

Born and raised in Pittsburgh, the Carnegie Library in Oakland was always my second home. I was diagnosed as being a high functioning autistic in college. I hold a useless double major in English literature and creative writing. I've worked at nonprofit agencies, in food service, and most recently as a dog-walker/pet sitter but the siren song of writing keeps pulling me back into its dark grip. I have co-authored a book on women in the US Senate with Billy Herzig, self-published *The Dog-Walking Diaries*, and in 2020 my first novel *Sarah Crow* was published by One Idea Press. I live in my hometown Pittsburgh with my better half, Smoky the Cat.

Email
wfrolik@hotmail.com

Facebook
www.facebook.com/wfrolik

Twitter
@wfrolik

Other NineStar books by this author

The Mary Gray Mysteries

The Illhenny Murders

Death at Bayard Lodge

A Swing of the Axe

CONNECT WITH NINESTAR PRESS

WWW.NINESTARPRESS.COM

WWW.FACEBOOK.COM/NINESTARPRESS

WWW.FACEBOOK.COM/GROUPS/NINESTARNICHE

WWW.TWITTER.COM/NINESTARPRESS

WWW.INSTAGRAM.COM/NINESTARPRESS

www.ingramcontent.com/pod-product-compliance
Lightning Source LLC
Chambersburg PA
CBHW070617100726
47907CB00007B/1777